WORLD LIKE A KNIFE

Johns Hopkins: Poetry and Fiction
John T. Irwin, General Editor

Fiction Titles in the Series

Guy Davenport, *Da Vinci's Bicycle: Ten Stories*
Stephen Dixon, *Fourteen Stories*
Jack Matthews, *Dubious Persuasions*
Guy Davenport, *Tatlin!*
Joe Ashby Porter, *The Kentucky Stories*
Stephen Dixon, *Time to Go*
Jack Matthews, *Crazy Women*
Jean McGarry, *Airs of Providence*
Jack Matthews, *Ghostly Populations*
Jean McGarry, *The Very Rich Hours*
Steve Barthelme, *And He Tells the Little Horse the Whole Story*
Michael Martone, *Safety Patrol*
Jerry Klinkowitz, *"Short Season" and Other Stories*
James Boylan, *Remind Me to Murder You Later*
Frances Sherwood, *Everything You've Heard Is True*
Stephen Dixon, *All Gone: Eighteen Short Stories*
Jack Matthews, *Dirty Tricks*
Joe Ashby Porter, *Lithuania*
Robert Nichols, *In the Air*
Ellen Akins, *World Like a Knife*

WORLD LIKE A KNIFE

Ellen Akins

The Johns Hopkins University Press
Baltimore and London

Stories in this collection appeared in slightly different form in the following periodicals, to which the author and the publisher extend their thanks: "Something You Won't Understand" and "Nobody's Baby" in *Southern Review*; "Her Book" in *Georgia Review*; and "Near November" in *Southwest Review*.

This book has been brought to publication with the generous assistance of the G. Harry Pouder Fund.

Printed in the United States of America

The Johns Hopkins University Press
701 West 40th Street
Baltimore, Maryland 21211-2190
The Johns Hopkins Press Ltd., London

The paper used in this book meets the minimum requirements of American National Standard for Information Sciences—Permanence of Paper for Printed Library Materials, ANSI Z39.48–1984.

Library of Congress
Cataloging-in-Publication Data

Akins, Ellen.
World like a knife / Ellen Akins.
p. cm.—(Johns Hopkins, poetry and fiction)
Contents: Something you won't understand—Nobody's baby—How easy it was—Blind instinct—The trouble with being right—3 A.M., your father—The easy version—Her book—Arriving in the dark—Near November.
ISBN 0-8018-4288-3.—ISBN 0-8018-4289-1 (pbk.)
I. Title. II. Series.
PS3551.K54W67 1991
813′.54—dc20 91-15802 CIP

Contents

WORLD LIKE A KNIFE

Something You Won't Understand

Mother had her baby in an alley, dropped it in a trash can. Troubled by little damage and some doubts, I rose from garbage and grew to womanhood, a forgiving sort of womanhood, for your sake. This will be the story of how I learned against the worst of odds what a woman can do and cannot.

And this is the story Mother told me when I finally found her: I thought you were dead, born dead after all I went through on your account before you were born, and I cried, oh I cried; for three days I was drowning in tears so I couldn't see.

Yes, and by then she could see through the mist that I was old enough to earn my keep and more, which is exactly what I had been doing since long before I was old enough—but I gave her the benefit and, for most of the time I was with her, liked a little the idea of having a mother for a mother.

Though she almost blinded herself again so happy was she at finally being found by her daughter, I became not her daughter but her sister as soon as I moved in, because by that time she was taking not offspring but money from men for her trouble—not in the manner of a whore, mind you. There is the business of my father, wherever and whoever he is, who is not, the story goes, a John. Mother, when I was her sister and daughter both, was more like a professional mourner than a whore. She talked with real tears about bad times and debilitating sickness befalling a host of relatives that, except for Papa-Grandpa, I never met, and men gave her money for everyone's relief. There was sex, too, but remember this: she liked it, or at least sounded to me like she did.

Enough about her. You'll want to know how I, stillborn to some, lived so long and fruitfully; if you don't, go ahead and sleep through some of what's to follow. When the story starts, my eyes are still stuck shut, but this much can be surmised from what I saw and heard and heard again and differently later: Being indisposed and a baby, I couldn't get out of my makeshift crib or do much else either, as you know too well babies can't, but had to be got out by someone—Maria Pio, from whom I spent most of my life running away or being stolen. Attached to my trash can was a restaurant, Pio's, a family operation where Maria cooked—she being a daughter to signore and a sister to most, and bringing out the trash she found me, didn't want me, but didn't know what else to do with me but take me out and take me in. She set me down and made me secure between two stacks of menus, then went to the ladies' room. While she was washing off the birth and Pio lettuce rot that must have clung to me and then to her, another Pio found me and took me to Grandpa Pio and said, What's this? or words to that effect. Grandpa Pio didn't know and said so, so the second Pio I'd been handled by wrapped me in a tablecloth and, like the family member and Samaritan she was, took me looking for the law. I can't tell you firsthand what happened while I was away, but here's a guess informed by my past and present: Maria, whose burden I'd become, in a moment of prescience, saw herself cheated out of the sixteen-year-long martyrdom of unwanted motherhood I was good for; thinking she'd been robbed, after her sister and like her sister, she went for the law.

Before either found a policeman, sister found sister and I changed hands. This is how I became Maria's. I was raised a Pio, named Pia, called Bimba, put to work on vegetables, sent to Saint Teresa's and told to be grateful, but I wasn't. Since Saint Teresa's, like the saint, was Catholic and unsuited to me in spirit and everything else, I concluded I was a Jew and persecuted, and ran away. I had advanced by then past the trash-can theory of conception, and so made my mother a Jew and made myself one, too, because I'd somehow conceived the notion that religion, like nationality, was a birthright. Later I found out that even if I'd been right about birthright, I'd have been wrong about mine because, as my mother, who believes in the birthright, told me without apologies, I wasn't Jewish or Catholic or anything but what I'd become.

I was a Pio and, as the family doctrine had it, there was something religious in that. Every time I ran away I was once more and worse a sinner, not in the Prodigal Son line, but unredeemable, only worth the bus fare it took to bring me back to guilt and shame and the cutting board. Every time I ran away, they found me, every time except the last. What I'm trying to say is this: I got a good, though interrupted, education. One time, A.W.O.L., I got as far as Kansas City, where I happened upon and to a guy who also had the habit of escaping, but who stayed away longer because the juvenile system was easier to hide from than the wrath of Pio, and with his help relieved myself of a few more things I wouldn't have to worry again about losing. But this guy was a bad provider of anything other than relief—early on we ran out of food and what we didn't run out of went bad in that hot basement and I got picked up at the store where I was picking up bread and cheese without paying. If I hadn't tried to manage some mustard, too, I would have made it and might be in Kansas City still. Be glad I'm a fancy eater.

Because I was a woman after Kansas City I started to understand some adult discussion I'd only heard in childish ignorance before that time. Other things I simply figured out and you will, too. First I wanted an answer to this: Why did Maria want to keep me when I hated her and she hated me but not enough to let me run away in peace? I inferred then that "Maria did the right thing" meant that Maria was an old maid from a young age because she believed in the wisdom of the antique expression "Why buy the cow when you can have the milk for free?" when "Why buy the cow when you haven't tried the milk?" is more like it. In her history there was a man, but Maria wasn't giving any teat, and the great romance that might have been and might have ended in marriage turned into a broken heart and bitterness before it even got started. There was another girl, Sophia Lido—she didn't do the right thing, and look at her. Sophia Lido gave and took a little bit too much and had a bellyful to show for it before, to the great relief of the Pios and their ilk, she went away and came back thinned-out to live in sin and shame.

So we come back, via my precocious intuition, to the Sophia part of the story, because it didn't take me long, only two years, to figure out that it was when Sophia got thin that Maria got me. I took off looking for Sophia Lido and found her three blocks away, living, I was surprised to find out but shouldn't have been, in the apartment where she'd been a baby and a kid my age and a pregnant disgrace, and subsisting, as I've said, on the graces of men, even, in a way, her father's—Grandfather's, Great-Grandfather's—because he stayed in the back room and collected pension checks, which stopped when he died while I was there. All the times I'd seen her but hadn't known her for my mother, maybe not all the times, gave us something to talk about and touch hands over the kitchen table over. This was after I spent an hour standing in the doorway relating the story of my birth as it had been handed down to me before she would let me into the hallway where she, whispering Bimba, Bimba as I spoke, listened to the rest.

These were the sleeping arrangements: Papa-Grandpa in the back, Sophia-Mother in the other bedroom, which was bigger and had once been the resting place for the parents, half of whom she'd relegated to the back, me on a sofa in the living room with a view of the kitchen before I closed my eyes. This was luxury, having a living room, because for sixteen growing years I'd split a twin bed with Maria until I grew so that we filled the bed so fully that just sleeping still as still could make us sweat from friction. Who knows what she did with the space once she had it to herself: hugged a side, my guess.

One night, awake with the noise of laughter not yet echoed out, I watched a man go searching through my living-room air for the door that he had many yards more to get to. Hey, I said, how's business?

For me, richer and poorer, he said, how's it with you?

I told him, Maybe now that I see magic fingers looking for the door and sleep coming, business'll be good. Then he laughed and fell on the door because he'd put his hands down.

I was working by that time at Eddie's, not Eddie's, the supplier for Pio's, but the other Eddie's, and every day had Mother appearing in my line to see if she could have me check her groceries through for free, which I didn't do, not once, because they keep an eye on you at Eddie's. There was Mother on the day after the unseen but heard drunken bedroom spectacle trying to coerce me with whispers into ringing up only every other item, which, again, I wouldn't do, but not because I didn't want to help my new-found family out, as I was doing anyway with my little income, and there outside Eddie's window was the businessman himself, not making any noise at all but walking arm to arm and almost hip to hip with my own Maria Pio. Mother, I thought, didn't see, but because I was looking out and not at her, there was some unaccounted-for looking time she might have used.

Mother cared about me more than for the benefits she never got, as I could deduce from a conversation, among others, we once had. But you ran away, she said, so many times.

It's just the kind of girl I am and school it was and house we had, not them at all, I said. They gave me room and board and moral absolutes to work with.

You wouldn't have, she said, rightful mother that she was, if I had known—not if I had known.

The specter of sentiment showed its face on hers and tears again were threatening so I patted her pretty hand and said, You did okay, what could you do?

Maria Pio did okay, she said, While I did nothing.

This might be a slight, I thought, but answered instead what might have been a sincere wringing of hands. Everybody did okay, don't cry, I said, We all got somehow through the worst of it and got the best out of it. I was being philosophical then, excuse me, but it convinced her and made her nod and stop that sniffling sound that I think should be saved for little animals because they haven't got our advantages.

The next day, after Eddie let me shed my smock and go, I got out to see, across the street and crowded about with passers-by, my two mothers, real and adoptive, standing face to face like a Sophia and Maria who had known each other long years ago. Or maybe for years—this was not a reunion with looks of surprise. The people who passed by passed more slowly when Maria and Sophia stopped bending heads together like old schoolmates and began to bellow in the low voices each of them had and saved for consummate emoting. Sophia slapped Maria. Maria returned the insult, but with the emotional flush of justness glowing on her abused face. I tucked my head and went for home at once, thinking there was going to be a fight or maybe that Maria, if she saw me, would try to get me back.

Thinking something, I went and must have arrived and left and come back late, for by the time I crawled into my sofa Mother's low voice of feeling was coming, mixed with man talk, under her bedroom door and into my living room, where it resounded around me and soon did a booming crescendo into the very tone Maria had heard earlier that day and probably the very topic, too. There followed, then, a racket that amounted in volume to the sound of every sheet slapping, every drawer and closet door banging shut. After a flash of yellow light, the door slammed on the businessman in question, who landed on the rug before me with a fit of muscle twitches, which is the symptom of a man not getting the last word. Standing there, he cast about and talked to himself, but very discreetly, while I watched. I backed myself into the cushion crevice so he could sit.

Your mother, he said, is a funny woman.

Mother? I said, She's my sister.

Sister, sure, he said, there's some things about her no one has to know.

This was not what I wanted to hear and, not about to, I eased myself out of the sofa crack enough to let him know that I was there. What? he said, lifting up my blanket, That's no way to sleep in Grand Central Station.

Sleep? I said, With all this noise? and did what I could to make him less sad than he might have been and not so talkative.

Sophia finally wondered what the man who hadn't come back in but hadn't gone out, not without his suit, was doing. There was no stopping what she discovered, so she sat in the armchair and cried us all to sleep.

A woman cannot be a mother and a sister or a mother and a lover or a sister and a daughter, for that matter. In the morning I was none of the above, but back, by daybreak, at the Pio's, where Maria, great-hearted with the righteousness of passive victory, took me in. Three months later, when my prodigality was proven, the family's Christianity reverted to its Old Testament beginnings and I was deprived of my place among Pios and put out. But, by then, neither the name nor the Pios were needed. You see, by the time it's got its own momentum from the accidental, incremental wisdom that life, in all its confusion, pushes through, a blessed thing cannot be helped and has to happen.

I didn't mean to have a moral or make a lesson out of what started as a simple bedtime story but got carried away into the closest thing to my life story we'll ever get. I just wanted you to know that however you're born and wherever you're put, a close sister of love will still be able to get you down and give you the next best thing to grace. But that's something you'll have to learn on your own, Sophia Pia Maria, because it's when you most need to hear something that you can't understand a word.

Nobody's Baby

Cold as it was, the girl would come down to George's wearing one of those summer dresses, little nothing, and as soon as she'd settled on her stool at the bar, one of the men would say, "Poor girlie."

"Ay," another would say, "got no clothes." And the rest would look sober, frown down for a second or two at their beers or their game, while Jack, wherever he looked, could see only the image invoked by those words. When at the end of the night he went home and fell into bed next to Lee, he would conjure the girl again, clothed, and then slowly take off that dress. Sometimes he did her a good turn, fended off one of his drunker companions or started her car when it stalled on the hill or carried her well water, and she took the dress off herself. The sight always shook him. He never got too far, barely touched the milky skin of her belly or thigh, before he woke up with his hands caught in Lee's nightgown. The one time he'd tried to kiss the girl good-night, she'd rebuffed him, but that might have been a dream, too. It would be hard to say. Sometimes in fact he woke up in the yard with no idea how he'd got there, curled up like a baby except for his work arm, which was thrown open behind him, dew on his hand.

The girl had been living in the woods above town for maybe five months when people began to notice her condition. As she walked down the street, the women would nod after her and say, "That's three months. Four at most." And the men, overhearing or told this directly, would dismiss the pronouncement with a soft "Nah," because the girl had turned back the advances of most of them and that was as many as had made advances and there was no one else around or they would know about it.

None of them had really tried that hard anyway—an offer to buy her a drink, drive her home, even walk her way up there, but that was all—because there was something fine about her that would have shamed them if they'd been any pushier. Whatever that something was, they'd sensed it even before she'd turned down the first of them, which accounted for the long time it had taken the first of them even to try. And then it became clear that she didn't need company the way they did, and this was assuredly a sign of something as well, which, because they didn't know what it could be, they figured must be above them, too.

So her pregnancy was perplexing, and sometimes when she sat on her stool now, with her back to the pool table, the men would consider each other at length, and, as soon as someone looked away, eyebrows would rise all around. Since the girl had out-and-out rejected them all and they were all there was, they'd come to the tacit conclusion that she'd been coerced, and, if not coerced outright, then tricked. They'd all done their share of tricking and fooling around and going too far, most often only in mind and if not then they owned up or else, which was why it seemed that the culprit in this case must have been a stranger—to them if not to her. Now, a stranger in town was a memorable event, so, once they gave it some thought, a few of them did seem to recall someone around about three months before, a man nobody claimed as a relative. He was tall, if they remembered right, with black hair and a hat, a fedora, and a beak nose. There the picture began to blur as they thought about it, one of them scratching his bald spot and one tucking in his shirttail and another tapping his flat teeth, and then they were all looking at Jack. He was tall enough and had black hair and what you might call a beak nose, but never in his life had he worn a fedora, let alone owned one. "What?" he said.

Roger said, "You were going to say something."

Jack said, "No I wasn't."

"Then why'd you clear your throat?"

"Can a man clear his throat?"

"It was the way you did it," Roger said, "Town-meeting fashion." The others nodded.

From behind the bar came George's dry voice, "That gal should go back where she came from." Everyone turned to stare as if he'd said, "She should be lynched." Then they were all looking at Jack again.

The next time the girl came to the bar, he sat at the far end of the counter, slouched to think and holding his head with his hand like a shade, until he was almost cross-eyed. When George stooped to glance up under his hand, Jack knew it had to be about last call, so he uncupped his nose and slid down off his stool and made his way along the bar toward the girl. Close enough not to be overheard, still he waited for the crack of the pool balls behind him before saying quickly, "Excuse me, Miss." Then he stuck. "I'm sorry," he said, "what's your name?"

This wasn't what he'd meant to say, but the girl had turned upon him her deep brown eyes. "You know it," she said.

It occurred to him that he must, though he couldn't remember at the moment just how he'd come by it or what it was. "Maybe so," he said, "but what I wanted to know is," he nodded, not wanting to point, and lowered his voice, "who's responsible?"

Her voice dropped, too, to that depth where he felt it before he heard, "Why don't you look in the mirror?"

To do so, he had only to raise his eyes. They met hers for a second, reflected, then he scanned the others, confused by her look and low voice until she clapped a five onto the bar and it all became clear. From a long way off, his image looked back at him like the real Jack, the girl walking away, the whole place silent for an instant.

There was that kiss. He went over it again, and then the way she'd pushed him off, and it pained him that he couldn't recall any more, though because the girl said so, he must be responsible—if not by due process, then by some other process involving his happiness in the grass and his guilt waking up with his wife. Marriage was responsibility; he'd always thought so, but never really felt it until the heat went out of his and that other warmth that was supposed to make up the difference failed to appear, and no children either to teach him and Lee something else about love, and now he was going to be visited with a baby after all, one who would grow up regarding him day in and out with strange eyes so that he'd finally know what responsibility really was.

Until three he wandered, sometimes stopping to retch, along the outskirts of town, where the last clipped reaches of grassy backyards verged on the weeds of the woods, and when he went home and Lee rolled over in bed to say, "You'll be in great shape at five," he was so sorry that he couldn't speak.

Every time he saw the girl after that, no matter how hard he tried to avoid it, she gave him a slow look so loaded with meaning that after a few times the weight almost hobbled him. Mother Nature put her in a superior position, and there she was, waiting to see who would be the first to say something—or would they have to wait till the baby could tell? This was a possibility Jack couldn't bear, so on a day when the girl had given him one more look as they passed at the post office, he made up his mind to speak.

That night he sat at the kitchen table long after he'd finished his dinner. When Lee hung up the dish towel and sat down across from him, he told her, "Get ready."

She said, "For what?"

"A baby," he said.

She said, "I've been ready."

"No," he told her, "that girl's. Baby, I mean."

Again she said, "What?" This time, however, she rounded the word out, making room for suspicion, and then snapped it shut.

"I never touched her that I remember," he told her. "Except to try and kiss her when I was too drunk to know better, let alone enjoy it, so I'm not even so sure about that. But she says the baby's mine, and it's my feeling she aims to give it to me."

Lee only looked at him, silent for so long, such a study, he started to wonder what else there was. Finally all she said, in a hard way she sometimes had, was, "She's putting you on."

He said, "No."

"And you never touched her."

"Except what I told you."

"So what makes you think?" She stopped there, but watched him for an answer anyway. After a minute, she threw up her hand as if to wake him, then, planting it on the table again, leaned in to say, "She'll bring that baby here over my dead body. Kisses or no."

At that, he started up from the table, so abruptly that he stumbled, astonished. "Where are you going?" Lee said, and he looked at her, sitting as fixed in her chair as an anchor. When he moved, her voice came after him, "Don't be a fool."

The girl lived on the point in a ramshackle cabin some said had been built by or belonged to her uncle, though no one knew him or anyone who'd ever lived there or in fact anything except that the cabin had somehow risen in a patch of woods forsaken by everyone but God and that girl. The light was so low by the time Jack reached it that he had to make three slow passes before he found the choked drive with, parked halfway down, her rusted white Honda, no bigger than a freezer box but still blocking the way, so he parked and walked.

Through the linty screen he could see a kerosene lamp on a table, where the girl sat, bent to read. As he put his hand on the knob, she said without looking up from her book, "Yes?"

He didn't know exactly what to say, so he waited there, hoping for help from the girl, who finally said, "You just don't give up, do you?"

"If that's mine," he said, again only able to nod, although he was standing in the dark. He was sickened to the point of immobility and hadn't even had a drink yet.

The girl sat back, crossed her hands on her belly, and turned her head to look at him, with a little glint—glasses, which he'd never seen her wear. Slowly she got up and walked over to where he was. "Christ," she said, peering at him through the screen, "you don't remember."

Jack bowed his head. "I don't remember anything," he admitted in a voice that almost disappeared.

"There's nothing to remember," she said.

Then he started to shake, and he couldn't stop, and he shook as if nothing but the cold were holding him together.

"Christ," the girl said again, plucking at his sleeve, "you'd better come in." He found it difficult to take a step. "Come on," she said, tugging, "you're letting the bugs in," and he let her lead him to the chair where she'd been sitting. Under his eyes was the book she'd been reading, *Your Baby and You,* which she slid away from him as he sat down.

Finally, when he could, he said, "I don't care."

"Don't care what?"

"Whose it is."

She was standing above him, studying him in a perplexed and skeptical way that reminded him of his wife, so he told her, "Somebody has to take care of it."

"Take care of it?"

"Sure," he said, "a baby."

"I thought I would do that," she said.

He said, "You?" Staring at her, feeling utterly blank, as if he'd shaken loose all of his sense, he said stupidly, "You're going to *keep* it?"

"You think I'd go through all this if I weren't?"

She shamed him into saying, "I guess not," but that was exactly what he'd thought—or, actually, he hadn't thought of the baby in any relation to the girl, except as something she'd been tricked into bearing until she could drop it on the life that, with its burdens and blind plodding, seemed to deserve it the most, and that seemed to be his, as he tried to explain. He told her he was staying put anyway, he had responsibilities, but she was free-floating, she came out of nowhere and went where she wanted and didn't need anybody, anybody could see, from the way she turned on his ear any man offering her a hand.

"A hand?" she said. "Don't need anybody? You think I only go down there because I need a beer? I'd go crazy up here alone." Now he was the skeptical one, thinking she was condescending to soothe him. Then she laid her hand on her belly and said, "But pretty soon I'll have company. That's my responsibility."

He felt no lighter for seeing the baby bound to the girl. In fact he felt as if he were weighing right down to the very depths where he could see what a burden it might be to watch someone at the beginning of a hard life like his. He said, "You said it was mine."

"I said look in the mirror. Anyway, you asked for it. You shouldn't go around thinking just because a woman's alone she might want you."

"I don't know why else."

Her smile was a wonder, even if it mocked him a little. "Who knows," she said. "Maybe there's something in that." As he stood up to go, she said, "Hey," and he turned. "If I do need someone—." And she patted her belly as if the baby might answer, although Jack was almost sure that by "someone" she meant him.

On his way back he stopped at George's, where over a beer he told the men that he'd just called on the girl and asked her point-blank: Who is it?

"Well?" Roger finally said for the rest.

"Nobody," Jack told them. "Can you beat that? It came on her like a dream."

Without lifting his head, George raised his eyes from the crossword puzzle he was working. "You see any proof?"

"Hell," Jack said, "she's carrying it around right in front of her, Georgie."

Late as it was, Lee was still up, sitting in front of the TV with the sound turned down. "Putting me on," he said, standing between her and the set. "You were right."

As if she were watching the silent show right through him, she stared at his midsection and said, "Let alone enjoy it."

That was her sole comment and, again, all she would say when he tried to get her to come to bed with him and all she would say later, too, when in his dreams he reached for her.

The girl had been living in the woods for approximately seven months when George called Jack to the telephone and, extending the receiver, announced for everyone's benefit, "Rachel."

Jack nodded as if he knew who that was, and then he recognized her voice, strained somewhat, saying, "I need someone now."

She'd driven as far as the gas station, where she'd had a pain and become afraid that she might not be safe driving the rest of the way. He took her to Mrs. Holman, the midwife, who turned as she was leading Rachel in and said to him, "Congratulations." Getting only a blank look in return, she said, "Daddy? I saw Lee yesterday."

This was news to him. What the midwife had seen of Lee had to be more than he himself had seen of her in the past few months, outside of his dreams. When? he wanted to ask the woman, how far along? but she was occupied with the girl, whose sudden shuddering pain unnerved him completely, so he started back to the bar instead, stopping at home on his way to look at Lee and see if he could tell, now that he knew, or maybe she would tell him. When he told her the news about Rachel, she said, "Premature?"

"No," he said, scrutinizing her, "right on time."

"You never can tell with the little ones," was all she said. This would be the women's explanation.

It wasn't until the next night that word came, from Holman arriving late at the bar. "Girl baby," he declared. "Seven pounds something." Jack sat there a while longer. Then, light-headed, he drifted in the direction of the midwife's, determined to ask about Lee so he would know just what to say to her.

He was standing in the walk leading to Holman's house, wavering, when a Buick drove up and a stranger got out. The man was short and stocky, gray-haired and wearing a fedora. Taking off his black gloves as he came, he paused before Jack, who was blocking the way, and asked in a soft, bass voice, "Is this the Holman residence?"

Jack stepped aside. When the man paused again and looked back, Jack said to him, "A man should look after his daughter."

"A man should mind his own business," the man answered, but Jack was already going, stumbling away in a hurry, looking for home. When he found it in an hour or so, he circled around to the back of the house and lay down in the patchy grass and slept without dreaming until the dew woke him.

How Easy It Was

He figured her for trouble from the first he'd heard of her, happy as he'd been for Mark, because the guy had had no luck with women for so long, eight years since the divorce and only two women that Tom knew of in all that time, plus one he suspected. His wife liked this new one, but she liked everyone, especially women out leading adventurous lives, pursuing goals, as she felt she ought to be, too, but wasn't, because her own goals weren't very well defined yet. So this Sandy, as the woman was called, appealed to her. She came from the city, where she lived in a converted piano factory and worked at the museum in an interesting job, the exact details of which Paula couldn't recall, although she remembered that they were impressive, and she'd invited her over for dinner. She'd invited Mark, too, but Mark was always invited. Paula hadn't known then that the two of them, Mark and Sandy, had already done more than meet, and they weren't letting on, but on the basis of a few subtle exchanges and looks over dinner Tom guessed how things were.

When he told Paula what he'd observed, she was skeptical but finally he was able to convince her and she acted pleased about Mark's sly success. But he noticed that she cooled considerably toward Sandy after that. This was perfectly understandable. Mark was their friend to a degree that made Paula a little possessive. In the absence of any woman in his life, she did a few feminine things for him, cutting his hair, sometimes making him dinner, watching movies with him that Tom didn't want to see, and the prospect of being needed less didn't sit well with her, he could see and had to admit he felt the same way.

There was also the question of what the woman was doing in town. First she'd come up for vacation, a long one, and stayed in a cabin her parents had built on the lake, and then she'd come back for another short stay, which stretched out longer and longer till a person had to wonder about her interesting job and adventurous life. She was around thirty, and it was Tom's guess that she'd exhausted the prospects back home and so had come up here where there were better pickings or at least better odds. Not that she had any reason to panic, looking like she did, and smart, but it happened to women; he'd seen it in Paula, who'd put off getting married and danced him around and then all of a sudden made up her mind as if somebody had tripped a switch. There were a lot of other reasons than men to like the area, nobody knew that better than Tom, but he didn't think a woman like Sandy, one who talked about art and wore dresses as a matter of course and mentioned two nights in a row the school where she'd got her master's degree, would care much for the quiet and the hunting and the camaraderie Friday nights at the bar—or, really, for the sort of people who lived here, not her kind at all. And, sure enough, as soon as she'd settled for more than a week, the men about town were ferreting her out and she was making fun of them.

Over for dinner again, she talked about Greg LeBeau, whose idea of courting was to come by and offer to chop wood for a girl and then ask if he could use her shower. The guy was an itinerant boatwright and Tom didn't have much use for him either, but when she described the way he'd showed her a stack of pictures of himself with boats, all of them dog-eared and some so out of focus as to be indecipherable, Tom felt bad at seeing such lonely guilelessness made to seem so shabby. Who knew what to do with a woman anyway? He couldn't exactly take her to the opera.

Tom said, "She can make fun of LeBeau. She's got something going with Mark."

"What?" Paula said. Now what she doubted was the depth of it. "Don't you think he'd tell us?"

Not with that one, he told her, Mark was hedging his bets. He had to be careful.

It was months later and Paula was still resisting the whole idea, saying Sandy was too foot-loose, not inclined at all to settle down—and she said this with admiration—when Sandy announced that she was moving in with Mark.

Tom wasn't surprised. A few weeks before, he'd gone over to get the two of them for a barbecue at the beach—he'd just walked in like he'd always done before Sandy's arrival—and found Mark and Sandy kissing in the kitchen, standing in the middle of the kitchen kissing so as not to notice someone walking in the back door, Sandy wearing a loose shirt that rode up, showing skin, when she reached her arms up around Mark's neck, and Mark with his hands on her back underneath, and it made Tom feel like he was sixty years old. There was never spontaneous kissing with Paula, let alone when someone might walk in, not since they'd got married, or even before. She had got restless, looking for her goals and seeing him as someone who didn't have any, although the truth was that he *had* his already, a house in the woods, a job that didn't kill him, softball and bowling and hunting and a woman like Paula, and she'd moved out for six months, which left him so lonely and confused that once she came back it just wasn't the same; he didn't know anymore what pleased her, since when he had thought he was making her happy, it turned out he didn't know what he was doing. Up till then he had been the fun one, the one girls went after, and she was the one who had been maybe a nerd growing up so she couldn't believe that somebody like him would want her, even after she'd outgrown the nerdy part and was everything anybody could want in a woman, mostly a good sport. But during those six months it seemed like Mark was the only thing they had in common. He'd wondered if something wasn't going on, but then she'd come back to him, and six more months later Mark was his best man. They'd never talked about it. He'd come back from driving his brothers to the airport after the wedding weekend and found Mark and Paula having a drink at the bar, and after he'd had a few beers himself he'd gone home to feed the horse and sat in the barn and cried like an idiot, knowing that Paula would never love him like she had once. What she loved was the fun guy she'd wished for when she was a nerd, and he wasn't that guy anymore. He was a man who had to go home and feed horses.

If anything, Mark was even farther from that mythical guy than he himself was. He was older and he had to pay child support and his job was harder on him—he was a builder in a place where there wasn't enough call for one, so he was always fixing porches and replacing doors and counters and never had the energy to work on his own house, which needed some work, even painting would help, but was always clean and tidy.

What Paula noticed first, when Sandy invited them over for dinner, was the new light fixture over the kitchen sink. Tom would never have noticed a detail like that, though he must have looked three or four times a week for six years at the bulb that Mark had had dangling there before Sandy started exerting her influence. In fact, when he thought about it, he preferred the bulb, and he said so. "It gave the place character," he said to Sandy, and she laughed.

"I can see I'm up against tradition," she said.

Paula said, "It's great. It changes the whole room." She said it with some vehemence, and he thought: Oh no. First the horses, which were hers, and now she would be wanting home improvements, although their house seemed good enough until Sandy came along. The trouble was, Paula wasn't such a good sport anymore.

Since she couldn't seem to fix on any far-reaching goals, she was looker closer to home and finding fault with this and that, setting goals for him instead, he thought, as if he wasn't the very same man she'd married for better or worse, let alone the same.

And once again, when they got home she said, "I can't see someone like her settling down."

In the remark he heard skepticism about settling down in general, Sandy being some kind of ideal. So he said, "Not everyone has to chase around to be happy."

"Isn't it chasing around," she said, "to come all the way here from Chicago to find Mark?"

That changed the subject because they agreed that Mark at least was worth chasing around to find, and the real question was, would someone like Sandy stick with him, or was he just a short-term goal? Paula said, "You could at least be nice to her." As if it were up to him. She always complained that he wasn't nice to her friends, and he tried to explain that he didn't know how to talk to women, to which she objected, first, that she, Paula, was a woman, wasn't she, and second, that you talked to women like you talked to men, but this he knew was just not true. You couldn't talk to women about the Civil War or World War II or football or baseball or hunting or town politics or in fact about anything, because they were different, they were intimate, they wanted to talk about something else, but for the life of him he couldn't figure out what and was struck dumb and nervous every time he tried.

"I *am* nice to her," he said, afraid he saw the general argument about women coming up again—but Paula got specific. She brought up his behavior at dinner that night, and, from the sound of it, he hadn't been particularly pleasant. He had had a few beers, so the incident wasn't altogether clear to him, but once she brought it up in detail he did remember the moment. He had been saying something about seeing one of his professors at a party, and Sandy had seemed bemused, had said her undergraduate classes had been so big that the idea of one of her professors even recognizing her was a joke. It was possible that he'd been confused. He'd thought she was saying that her school was something and his, the local college, was nothing. It was the "undergraduate" that got him. So he had started saying where his professors had come from, one from Harvard, one from Penn, and so forth, that's how *small* it was, until he'd realized that all of them, Mark and Sandy and Paula, were staring at him as if he'd just fallen off the moon.

It would be the first time he had to talk alone with Sandy,

because he did agree with Paula that he should apologize. When Paula got irritated she wouldn't even let him touch her. The next day, he stopped over and Mark's kids were already there for the weekend, so he took Sandy into the only private room, the bedroom, which he realized immediately was a mistake, one only he could make, because he was so good at putting women and their intimate ways out of his mind. Sandy seemed a little baffled. He told her what Paula had said and how he saw that he hadn't been nice and he was sorry. She said she thought it was the beer, and he told her that it wouldn't happen again, and then she kissed him on the cheek and he had to get out of there.

Mark said, "What was that about?" amused but without a hint of suspicion, which was appropriate, just the way Tom had been when Mark and Paula had spent so much time together during the six months of trouble. They were friends.

After such an effort on his part, he couldn't figure out why Paula wasn't doing the same, because it was easier for her anyway, talking to women. All of the women seemed to be pulling away. When Sandy had first shown up, they were all nice to her, as they were to anyone new who wasn't strictly a tourist, but then, as soon as she started to settle in, it was like they all remembered that they'd been there for years together and had more in common with each other than with a stranger, no matter how interesting. So he asked Paula, "Why don't you do anything with Sandy anymore?"

"She's so wrapped up with Mark," she said, "and besides, I don't think she understands our friendship. I mean, she might resent it, since we go back so far and she's so new. You know, the territorial thing." This was news to him; she could talk about "the territorial thing" and then tell him he had to talk to women.

He could see how Sandy could get lonely and start missing her museum and her friends and then who knew what would happen, so, for Mark's sake, he tried to be nice to her, though sometimes the woman made it difficult. For instance, when she saw the bear in the back of his truck, what she said was, "It's so little!" like he had gunned down a puppy or something, when the bear was more than a yearling by a long shot and, besides, he had had a perfect shot at a huge bear but when he saw her cubs he couldn't make himself shoot, something a man couldn't tell anyone, except Paula, who was sworn to secrecy.

Even though her tone stung him and made him *want* to say something about the big bear, when she added, "But it's better than shooting a mama," he was furious. What else was Paula telling her?

She had the manner of a someone who thought she knew that a man's life wasn't perfect, though he wasn't complaining. He had only asked Paula to be a little nicer to him in public. That was all. They'd gotten into a routine, so long ago that he didn't remember when, where he would nuzzle up to her and she would act like he was so annoying that he was forced to be even more amorous, which made her more combative, and so on, and lately he had seen how it might have gotten out of hand. Watching Mark and Sandy he had seen how, if people thought this was the way a happy couple acted, then they might misunderstand the way he and Paula played around. Whether this was what gave Sandy the wrong impression or whether Paula had been making confessions, by way of trying to be nice again, he didn't know, but he would swear the woman was acting sorry for him.

She even asked him over to watch football. What she said was, "I'll probably be out working in the yard," and he was aware of everything in the exchange, that he had left his friend Mark so much alone that she was forced to ask him over to watch the game, along with the hint that she was the reason he didn't come over so much anymore.

He said, "You could watch the game." After all, she did come from Chicago, and the Packers were playing the Bears. It *was* a game that he really wanted to see, and they didn't have a television; Paula thought TVs were a bad influence.

She said, "Maybe I will."

The surprising thing was, she did. It was the worst game in the history of football. Mark was only in and out, working on the heating, now that he was getting rid of the wood stove, because it turned out Sandy was allergic to the smoke. "This wasn't my idea," she said to Tom, sounding sorry at the racket of Mark drilling in the other room, which made the picture staticky, but what else could a man do? Paula complained about their wood stove, too, but her complaints were easier to ignore, because he couldn't do this kind of work; and anyway, he liked having the stove there when he came in cold or with his boots wet, he liked splitting the wood, he liked the homestead feel of it.

They were sitting next to each other on the sofa, the only way for both of them to see the set straight on, though he wouldn't have minded moving to the armchair, at an angle, once she sat down next to him, but once she had sat down he couldn't, knowing how that would look, like he wasn't being nice to her, so there they were. She was wearing a sweatshirt and jeans, a change he noticed, although Paula said he never noticed clothes, not his or hers or anyone's, and so she was proved wrong. He also noticed, when she turned to talk to him about the safety—in the Packers' end zone, of course, his hopeless team falling apart in what, from his point of view, was stacking up to be a stomping of his team by hers, which she didn't even notice, because all she seemed to care about was somebody coming from behind, making a surprising move, it didn't matter who—when she turned, touching his leg, he noticed that Mark's sofa wasn't in great shape. Before Sandy showed up, it would never have occurred to him to notice the condition of Mark's sofa. She was looking where he looked, so he said, "Kind of worn, hunh?" and then he felt just terrible, like it was something against Mark he'd said. "But comfortable," he added. "That's what counts. This place was always comfortable." That was worse. He could have kicked himself for saying "was," even though he didn't mean a thing by it, for instance, that it wasn't comfortable anymore.

It must have been five minutes later, right in the middle of a crucial play, when she said, "Listen, Tom, I don't want to come between you." At first he thought she meant Paula. Then she said, "I'm trying not to, but I don't know what to do."

The confusion that this caused him was impossible because on one side he thought she was right, she was wrecking his friendship with Mark, and on the other he thought it was presumptuous on her part to imagine that someone so new could come between two friends who went back so far, and then he thought it was his fault because he was so bad with women, especially pretty women who were nice to men in a way that he wasn't used to and never would have thought to miss if Sandy hadn't come along, and wasn't it high time that Mark had a woman being nice to him, and then it seemed like Paula's fault. Why did she have to hate the N.F.L.?

"It's just winter coming," he said. "Things always change around here at this time of year." But he could still feel her looking at him, turned, with her knee touching him. "It's me, he said. "I'm weird. I'm no good with women."

She said, "But if it were Mark and you and Paula, it wouldn't be like this. It would be okay."

"Because of me," he said, "that's why. Because Mark's good with women. And it's different. It's like—." He stopped, feeling stupid, but she was still watching him, waiting to hear. "It's like we were kids," he said. "I don't know what happened. I don't think it's you."

"Whoa!" Mark whooped, coming to the door behind them. They'd missed the most amazing pass. He bent over the back of the sofa on the other side of Sandy to kiss her, and when she leaned back under the pressure she squeezed Tom into the corner of the sofa, so he could hardly breathe. There he'd been, telling her something difficult because she asked, missing the most amazing pass, and already she'd forgotten, already she was kissing Mark as if to prove that some women were affectionate in public.

As soon as Mark went back to work, she turned to Tom and said, "I wish I knew how to do whatever it is he's doing. This makes me feel so guilty."

"Mark's a big boy," he said. "He wouldn't do it unless he wanted to."

That week, he decided, he would start to make a special effort. He would stop by after work, the way he used to, and would visit with them. He would not avoid looking at her, as Paula said he did, and he would include her in everything he said. But when he got there he discovered that Sandy had gone back to Chicago for a few days to see friends, so it was a wasted effort. And when they tried to talk about the game he was embarrassed that Mark seemed to know more about it just from reading the paper than he did after watching it on TV.

"When's Sandy coming back?" he asked.

"On Sunday."

"Hey, then we can batch around on Saturday."

"If you want to batch around here," Mark said, "I have to get this work done. Where's Paula?"

"On some sailing trip out to Isle Royale."

"In this weather?"

Tom shrugged and then they both laughed, because they knew Paula so well and it was just like her to make a supposed pleasure trip in the freezing wind. Then suddenly they weren't laughing anymore, they weren't saying anything, and the silence went from companionable to awkward, at which point Tom announced that he had better go throw some wood on the fire.

At home he hunkered by the wood stove, warming himself, feeling how nice it was to know where the heat came from in a house, like a heart that you could touch and know that it was working. Having the house to himself, he thought about his friends from school, the ones he could call up to play a game of cards or have a beer, but one by one he saw them sitting down to dinner or beached in front of a TV or putting kids to bed or going to bed themselves, tired from one long workday and getting ready for another, and so he wandered away from the stove, looking for books that he'd been meaning to read. There was a book about the Yankees, he didn't know where he'd put it, and he thought about Lou Gehrig, saying he was the luckiest man on earth when he was just deteriorating. The man was so heroic, it choked him up, and, when he thought about it, Mark was like Lou Gehrig, not that he was deteriorating, but in his attitude, how happy he always was with what he had, no matter what that was, how he had been alone for all those years and seemed happy enough while everybody else had to have company like a crutch. He, for instance, had to have Paula, had to have Mark. If he were to get a disabling disease he knew he wouldn't consider himself lucky, although of course he'd never played for the Yankees; but in the same situation Mark would probably say that he had had it good.

On Sunday he had cleaned the house because Paula would be coming back from her trip to Isle Royale. She was always happier after one of her adventures, and he liked to hear about it, just to see her so excited, full of stories of the mishaps and near misses that always occurred when she went anywhere with her sporty friends. He wanted Paula to have fun, but sometimes she didn't think so, sometimes she thought there was only so much fun to go around, which meant that if she was having it he wasn't and to tell him about it would be rubbing it in or, worse, it would be like admitting that it was his turn now, since he'd missed out on so much, although that wasn't how he thought about it, not at all. He didn't want to capitalize on her fun, on her high spirits. The only problem was, there was no other time; there were only high spirits or low, and better high spirits than low, was how he thought, but still the time never seemed right. He got so nervous waiting that he finally gave up and went to Mark's.

Sandy let him in. "You're back," he said, and she said, "What about it?" and he laughed, but only after the minute it took him to realize that she meant her back, what about it? By then she had sat down again at the kitchen table, where she'd been reading a book. He stood in the middle of the room, feeling that something wasn't right. "Where's Mark?" he said.

"In the crawl space," she said, "plumbing." Then she buried her face in her book as if she were going to sleep, but in a second or so he could see that she was crying, and he started to feel desperate, a panicky feeling that crying always brought out in him.

"Hey," he said softly, treating the tears like a secret so as to make them go away, "hey, hey," and he went over and put his hand on her shoulder. Now she was truly shaking with the misery of it, whatever it was. "Hey," he said, "what's the matter? It's okay."

"It's so stupid," she said into her book so he could barely hear. "I know he's doing this for me, but I can't help it, I feel, I just."

"What?" he said. He gave her shoulder an encouraging squeeze. The thing about crying was, it made him feel much clearer about women, because there was only one way to act, and that was helpful.

Then she turned her head and buried her face in his shirt, waist-high, like a child, because she was sitting down. "Abandoned," she said. "He's either working down there or he's tired, and I feel like it's my fault."

Patting her back as he was now, he could feel her calming down, her breath coming less ragged against his stomach, too, where it was making a warm spot. "It's okay," he said again, "it'll be done pretty soon." But that only brought on more shuddering, like she was crying harder, though he couldn't tell because she was so muffled up against him.

"I know," she said, it sounded like, the saddest sounding words she'd said.

Suddenly he was aware of how the hand she'd slung around his back had become still. It had been closing and opening with her sobs, grasping handfuls of his coat, but now it wasn't anymore, a sign that she was finished crying and trying to figure out how to get out of this. He eased away. It took her a few seconds to look up, and, when she did, he said, "Are you okay?"

She said, "I'm sorry."

He made a motion with his hands, a shrug to tell her to forget it. Already he was embarrassed, now that her face wasn't hidden, so he said, "I won't go down there if he's working. You can tell him I came by."

She said, "Are you sure?"

"Yeah," he said, "I've been down there. I'm not up to crawling around now."

It was just like a woman, wasn't it, he thought, walking away. A man did what he could to please her, and it only made her more unhappy. Still, there was something funny about it. Hadn't she spent weeks at a time at her parents' place out on the lake and never cried about being alone, although of course he wasn't sure, not having known her then, but wasn't that the impression Paula had got, that Sandy on her own was fine? But maybe she had gotten used to Mark, the way that he was getting used to her and wouldn't be the same if he was left alone again. The spot where she had breathed into his shirt turned cold out in the wind, and he zipped up his coat.

What struck him as he went into the bar to get a beer was how this came right after her trip to Chicago. What occurred to him was that she'd come back from her friends in their piano factories only to find out that it wasn't the heating she missed. With the beer the warmth was coming back to him, hitting him again right in the middle, as he heard over and over Sandy saying into him, "I know."

All week he stayed away. After going through that scene, he was embarrassed about facing Mark, feeling that a man should say something and all the same wondering what, wondering if to say something would be a breach of confidence, or then again was it a breach of confidence for Sandy to cry to him in the first place? It might be that most women were like Paula after all, confessing everywhere but at home when they weren't happy. Even when Paula went down to trade adventure stories with Sandy, he didn't go along. Let the women talk, he thought, let them compare notes. Let them tell each other how men always ended up being no fun. And if Mark wanted to join in, then let him, let him contribute a word or two about how his old friend Tom had disappointed his old friend Paula, because he was in a position to know. Then let him remember how much fun his old friend Tom had been before all that, before the six months of sleeping around that Paula needed to decide that sex wasn't everything, it wasn't the most important thing, it wasn't even important.

At last he went down there alone, again on Sunday, and again Mark wasn't there, not even in the crawl space this time, but Tom found he was embarrassed anyway, facing Sandy, after seeing her in tears. Mark was out of town, she said, gone to get some fittings that he needed for the heat. Feeling that it would be rude to leave as soon as he heard that, Tom stood in the kitchen searching for something to say. She was standing a few feet away from him, the step or so she'd taken from the table as she'd told him to come in. Finally he said, "Are you okay?"

"Yes," she said. "Are you?" As she said it, she took a step closer, so the concern in her voice and eyes seemed to be rushing at him.

"Why wouldn't I be?" he said, and she lowered her eyes, just for a few seconds but long enough for him to see that he was the one moving. He was closing in on her. "Why wouldn't I be?"

"I don't know," she said. She looked him full in the face, and he felt something inside him give. "I thought." But that was all she said, and the next thing he knew he was kissing her, he had his arms around her, and her body pressed against him, bringing on that powerful feeling that made him helpless. It was like hunting, the compulsion, just like with the bear. I knew it, he was thinking, but he couldn't stop it. I knew it, he was thinking, then not thinking anymore until he had her on the sofa, clinging to him like somebody falling, holding on so tight that at the last sorrowful moment he had to remember how it felt to have someone who loved him cling to him like that, how easy it was. This was all he wanted, this was all, and if it was so unimportant, why couldn't it be easy, like this?

Because she's no good, he was already saying to himself, just like I thought, and, if this is all I want, then maybe it's all I deserve. Already it didn't look so easy anymore. No good, he kept telling himself, no good, and now she'll go away and everything'll be the same again, but that was no good either. She could go away or stay, but he would still have to go home and get what he deserved, nothing, now that they were even, now that he and Paula could agree on what was not important without ever saying a word, and then they could take up Mark again and be like kids again with him between them, lucky as Lou Gehrig.

Blind Instinct

Touching the fat purple edge of her eye, she thought: What else? A black eye. It made sense. Her eyes were the only feature in her face that kept her from being pretty—tolerable, anyway. They were dark and sunk deep, as if they'd never grown out to where they were supposed to be, and in pictures taken of her in the sun, what her dad called the Cro-Magnon series, you couldn't see them at all for the shadows. If it weren't for her eyes, as she saw it, a man might be satisfied just looking at her once he got through with character and had to have something to look at, when looking was all that was left.

Character didn't keep. She knew it firsthand. Even with men, who could sometimes get away with character instead of looks, sooner or later you would notice something, nose hairs or blotches or moles shaped like some foreign country. Sometimes what struck her was something as obvious as a nose that she'd never noticed stuck out so far, and that's when she knew she was through looking into a man. She'd looked till she'd found something else, plain as a nose, to fix on, just as a man, when he'd seen enough character, fixed on her eyes—as Joe did, until he got frustrated, because eyes were harder to stare down than a nose.

Then he went to the bar to get away. She knew just the one. Thinking that if she went there like this, people would stare and think what they thought as a rule about beat-up women, which she wasn't, she tried hiding the bruise with make-up. That only made it look worse, fat but not purple, like something from birth, so she wiped off the make-up and put on her sunglasses. In the mirror, in the low bedroom light, they looked black. They hid everything. Someone seeing her wearing these glasses at night might wonder if she had a black eye but wouldn't know and might as well guess she was shy or famous or extra sensitive to light.

But outside, because the glass filtered out everything except streetlights and headlights, she couldn't tell what people guessed when they passed. They could think she was ridiculous and she wouldn't be able to see it in their faces. With her nerves starting up like the buzz of a timer before it went off, she looked straight ahead and walked fast until she got to the bar, where the light was so dim that she had to slow down and concentrate on not knocking into anyone on her way to the table she wanted. It was close to the bar but not too close, and, sitting with her back to the wall, she could see the door well enough to watch for Joe without making a point of it.

As soon as she had her chair arranged and was sitting still her nerves started up again. She sat there, stiff, listening to the buzz, until it occurred to her that what she heard was only the hum of the bar, just as it was when she'd walked in the door. The noise of the voices and glasses and bodies in motion was steady. She settled back, and it seemed to recede. While she watched, dim outlines filled with features, mouths around words, hands shaping gestures, like a TV warming up on a show, and, observing it all from behind her dark glasses, she felt almost as invisible as she was to the people she watched on the Zenith at home.

Then she noticed a boy two tables down looking at her. He glanced past his friends, quick and shifty, the way people at a party snuck looks at someone standing around with a camera. Sliding her eyes to one side then the other, she caught the same look from an old man sitting slouched at a table and then from a man standing up at the bar, and there was no way of knowing how many glances she'd missed while she was busy being invisible.

The man at the bar looked around again, smoothing a few hairs sideways across his bald spot as he told the bartender something. When his eyes reached her he stopped with his hand flat on his head and his mouth stuck for a second in the slack *O* of whatever he'd said—just one struck second, and then he picked up his drink and looked at that.

In that second she thought she'd been stupid; she was just as strange in sunglasses as with a black eye. But watching the balding man at the bar, seeing how short his look at her was and how nervous, just like the boy's, she saw her mistake. They weren't staring at her. In fact, they were looking like people stared at. The man at the bar made another remark and glanced around when the bartender ignored it or just didn't hear, which was the man's problem, along with his lack of hair. Behind her glasses, she shifted her eyes back to the boy, who was listening to the others with a troubled smile, as if he didn't understand a word they said. And the old man? Maybe his oldness alone was making him insecure, though there might have been something else, a secret he thought someone staring could see. None of them could tell if she was looking or where, so they all just assumed she was staring at them. Everyone, she thought, is hysterical.

It gave her a feeling of power, a generous feeling, so that when the bald man turned and stared toward her she wanted to tell him not to worry, all she saw was a middle-aged man who was losing his hair, nothing strange. His big body dwindled down to tiny feet, and he walked like a burglar in a cartoon, head first and hunched and almost on tiptoe when he raised himself sideways to fit between two tables. He stopped right in front of her, blocking her view of the door, so she gave him a hurried "Hello?" then was sorry at once that she'd sounded impatient, because he'd fallen back a step. He could only see her good features, she reminded herself.

"Do you mind if I sit?" the man asked.

She said, "No," then she added, "that is, I don't mind," and he sat right where she could look at him and watch for Joe, too. He unbuttoned his jacket and smoothed his bald spot and crossed his legs in a particular way, all the time taking quick looks at her, till she started to think that she ought to take off her glasses and show him that she wasn't studying him for a fault. But just then he jumped up again and asked her if she wanted a drink. A beer, she said, sure, and he hurried away, looking relieved or maybe even grateful.

The man hunched at the bar while he waited, his shoulders bunched up, nearly hiding his head, and his elbows stuck out like the wings of a big sitting bird. Watching him come back with his arms still like that, the bottle and glass in one hand on his belly, she felt sorry for him, the poor man, spending half his sight looking back at himself through somebody else's eyes. She knew how it was and she reached for her glasses, but stopped with her hand in the air when he bent with the beer and let her see Joe coming in the door.

He saw her, too. Only someone who'd watched him as closely as she had would notice the hitch the sight of her put into his walk, it was so subtle. Then he went on walking straight to the bar. That was Joe; his thoughts ran like an electrical current, and the most anyone on the sidelines could expect was sparks. Try to cut in, and you got a shock.

The bald man had put her glass into her hand and gone back to his side of the table, where he was sitting now, still hunched and wearing that look that was nervous and eager, as if he were Mr. Budweiser himself. So when she sipped, she gave him a smile. "Did you ever hit a girl?" she asked him.

It took him a second, and then he said no.

"You didn't," she said. "Did you ever want to?"

Faster this time, he told her no again. She said, "Don't get upset. It's natural, you know."

"I don't know what—" he said, and she told him, "The instinct to fight. It's a natural instinct."

"It may be natural," the man said, "but—."

"What what? I know, we have to show restraint. Otherwise everything would be a brawl with nothing getting done, everybody knows that. Natural, you said, but look how you got your back up when I asked you."

He started to protest, and she said, "See? A man's not supposed to have the instinct when it comes to a girl. Not even the instinct, forget the restraint. But it's natural, isn't it, didn't you say? A man can't help that. Natural, but it's not supposed to be there, so when it is, it's like the girl shows a man he's not as civilized as he's supposed to be, so he holds it against her and balls up inside till he has to hit out and it's not from the instinct at all. It's like hitting himself."

She was taking in her normal voice, but she knew Joe could hear. When he listened without looking, he tensed up his back and his neck, like a cat at first sight of something suspicious.

Leaning in close to the table again with his shoulders rolled up, the man nudged her hand with her beer and said, "Well, I'm a man and—."

"I know," she agreed. "It's easier on some people. Restraint, I mean. You might not even know it. But let me tell you, I've seen it all my life. Even when I was a kid—there was a boy, for instance, in fifth grade, and he just bothered me. Always making faces and nasty remarks for no reason at all, so I did it back, the same thing. And then one day he poked me." She jabbed the air to show him how vicious it was. "Like that, and then he just stood there. This close. So I went—." She flapped her hand at an invisible face. "Then I went—." She nudged it with her knuckle.

In his soft voice he said, "Were you born—."

But she finished her point, "And then," and she jabbed the air again, harder this time. "And he socked me so hard I couldn't breathe, you know, like when the wind gets knocked out of you. And there he was then, I'm telling you, *crying*."

Joe jerked a dollar out of his pocket and slapped it onto the bar. She started to stand, but the bald man jumped up so fast when she moved that he knocked his chair into the table behind him, and she dropped back into her seat for a second, surprised.

On his way to the door, Joe slowed for a step, and the man pulled out her chair for her. Then she tried to get up again, but he leaned down and got in her way, reaching for her elbow and sliding his other arm behind her. With his grip fixed on her elbow, he lifted, saying softly into her ear, "Here you go," as if she were an old lady or crippled or, she thought: blind.

She wrenched her arm free and her chair hit the wall. She grabbed the sunglasses off of her face. "What do you think?" she hissed at him. "I'm *blind?*"

Everyone was looking at her. They were staring at her eye. "He did this!" she said. She said, "You!" and she pointed with her finger shaking and her eyes stinging in the sudden sharp light.

Joe came over slowly and stopped at her hand. He rolled her fingers into a fist and folded her arm and wrapped his hand around her elbow. His hold was as helpful and firm as the man's, but Joe knew better than to try and move her. He waited for her to move. "It's just my eye, you idiot," she said. "My leg's not broken. That's what you wish you did, isn't it? Broke my leg, and then I couldn't come here." She blinked up at him. "You're sorry now, aren't you?"

"Yes," he said. There was that hitch that only she could see. "Yes I am," he said, and she could see that he was, and so, with him holding her elbow, she allowed herself to be moved.

The Trouble with Being Right

Out of kindness she'd reviewed that sad business, the Hacienda House, a restaurant she might have ignored, as most people in town seemed to do. The décor was pleasantly kitschy, she'd written, the service speedy (no mention of how little the waitress and cook had to do) and the fare for the most part above par, though the taco had been somewhat greasy. On the night the review appeared in the paper, she was glancing over the text when the telephone rang.

"Kay Jackson? Who writes for the paper?" a woman's voice asked in peremptory fashion. "This is Dinah Johnson. Who owns the Hacienda House." Kay waited, and in a while the woman added, "Which you reviewed."

Kay said, "Yes?"

Again she waited. Finally the woman spoke. "Grease is a matter of opinion," she said.

"Grease is?" Kay said. "Maybe degrees of grease, but not grease itself. That's a fact." The woman said nothing. Concluding that she was unhappy with the review and simply wanted reassurance, Kay told her, "A review is a matter of opinion, though, and people know that. Anyway, it was a pretty good one, all in all."

"*For the most part,*" Dinah Johnson said, her voice flat, each word laid down like the last. "You irresponsible spoiled social creature, I want you to write a retraction right now."

It took Kay a minute to convince herself that she'd heard this right. "I'm not an irresponsible spoiled social creature, whatever that is," she said. "And I'm not about to write a retraction."

"Maybe you need time to think about it."

"No, I don't. It wasn't a bad review, the paper wouldn't print a retraction, and I stand by what I said anyway. I'm sorry."

"You will be," the woman said and hung up.

Now Kay began to wonder why she'd ever bothered to review that place. So much for civic duty. The telephone rang and she picked it up sharply and snapped out, "Hello."

"What did I do now?" It was Lou, a man she'd been seeing. She told him about the exchange with Dinah Johnson, but he only chuckled.

" 'You'll be sorry,' " she said. "That could be a threat."

Lou said, "What else could she say?"

It was a point. A psychiatric social worker, Lou knew about threats, he knew about stress, he spoke with authority about "venting"—so she curbed her impulse to call the police and settled down again with the papers she'd been grading.

Within a half-hour she'd become so engrossed in her work that the sound of the doorbell gave her a start. Standing on the step were the Lupresto twins, Tommy and Billy, who'd come to see about mowing her lawn. Like most of her neighbors, she didn't trust the boys, so she hired them to do yard work once or twice a week, in the hope that a contractual arrangement would prevent them from robbing her house. This time, however, because they'd mowed the lawn only three days ago, she told them to come back some other time.

Kay had just about forgotten Dinah Johnson's call by the next evening, when the telephone rang. "Did you think anymore about retracting?" that flat voice demanded. Kay was silent, and after a moment the woman went on, "You ruined my business."

With great effort, Kay adopted a reasoning tone. "There were only two other customers the night I was there."

"I know. That was a slow night."

"It was Friday."

"Yes, Friday."

"Friday's generally a busy night for restaurants."

"Not mine. For mine it's a slow night, I remember saying."

After another inexorable silence, Kay said, "Miss Johnson, I don't think I could possibly ruin your business. And even if I could, that review—"

"Ms."

"Ms. Johnson—that review wouldn't have done it. I'm sorry if you're having trouble, but I—."

"Is that it?"

"It?"

"Your answer?"

Her tone was so ominous that Kay was searching nervously for something else to say, when the woman hung up.

Then Lou stopped over and she made the mistake of telling him about this development, a mistake because she knew what he'd say, with his gift for sympathy. "Don't you think you might be overreacting?" he said.

"No, she is."

"No, she's boxed into a corner. She's letting off steam."

"Most things boxed into a corner bite."

As if at a cue the Luprestos' dog barked, and Kay leapt up to look out the window. "Kay," Lou said, "Kay," putting his arm around her and easing her down to the sofa again. "I work with troubled people all day, I'm telling you, it's okay." Then she heard the burr of the Luprestos' motorbike and tried to rise again, but he held on to her, saying, "Speaking of which."

"What?"

"Your twins." He tipped his head. "Isn't that their bike?"

"They're not my twins. What about them?"

"Talk about troubled," he said. "Someone at Cardinal told me they checked in last weekend."

"Cardinal?" Kay was incredulous. It was a sanatorium of sorts, where the town's disturbed, elderly, chronically ill, convalescent, battle-weary, and bored went for "time out" and sometimes for good.

"I guess someone convinced the one—Tommy?—that he needed help. Then the other one—."

"Billy. Tommy gun, billy club."

Lou grimaced at this characterization. "Billy tried to check in, but the staff thought that might be—counterproductive. So Tommy decided that kind of help he didn't need and snuck out, pretending to be his brother, not that he had to sneak out, but you know, the romance: They made a getaway. In their dad's car, which they raced around until the poor guy had to report it stolen so he could get it back and get to work. But I heard they ran out of gas anyway, before the cops found them. So they got a ride home."

He squeezed her hand. "Sweet kids," she said.

"They *are.*" He put his arm around her. "Just mixed up. And you're just worked up."

"I'm not troubled people," she told him.

"I didn't say that. 'Worked up,' I said. But I'm here."

He was so understanding. The thought was just pointed enough to needle her conscience into wondering: What was wrong with that? Here she was, living an imperfect yet quite decent life, and she wanted more sympathy than two disturbed teen-agers or the poor owner of a failing business or all those other pathetic people Lou ministered to. She leaned against him, a little sorry but still suspecting that she deserved sympathy, if only for her perplexing uncertainty as to why.

When he left, late as it was, she drove to the Hacienda House, not knowing exactly what for—a talk, perhaps. But as long as she watched, until they closed at one, she couldn't see anyone, other than the waitress, who seemed attached to the place; or any customers.

In the morning the hood ornament, the truncated peace sign, was missing from her Mercedes. Someone had viciously twisted it off. The Mercedes was a decrepit old relic, beaten and battered, but just the sort of car that, in full polished paint and good repair, a spoiled social creature might drive: This had occurred to Kay by the time she'd backed out of the garage.

Spotting Tommy Lupresto on his motorbike, she flagged him down to ask him if he'd seen anyone around her house this morning or last night—a strange woman, maybe? Billy came up behind his brother, and, though he hadn't heard the question, the two of them looked at each other then back at her with an expression she'd seen on her students when they knew an answer but didn't want to give it. "I'll pay you," she said. "If you keep an eye out for anything funny."

Tommy pushed his hair back off his forehead and looked at his brother, who said, "Ha-ha," and cocked his forefinger at her in what she could only assume was a sign of agreement.

When she got to school there was a note in her box: Dinah Johnson. Seeing her glance up from the slip, the secretary told her, "That's it. She said she'd catch you later."

Kay called the newspaper. She spoke to her editor. Yes, he said, he'd given her number to someone that morning. When Kay told him about Dinah Johnson, the man emitted a comical sigh. "Ah, the liabilities of the critic," he said.

"She pulled the hood ornament off my car."

"Kay," he said. "Really. The woman who called didn't give the impression of a vandal."

"What, you did a psychiatric evaluation? Of course she didn't give you that impression. She wanted the number. She's crazy. She's crafty. She's after me, Norm."

"Take a deep breath, my dear. Collect yourself. Nobody takes those reviews seriously."

She hung up on him.

Her students, ever sensitive to mood and nuance, were dull and uncompliant all day, and she ticked off the minutes until she could go to the lounge and relax, maybe tell one of her colleagues about her predicament or bury her anxiety in a book. But when she finally was free, there was no one else in the lounge and, try as she might, she couldn't concentrate enough to read. Still trying, suddenly she thought she saw the waitress from the Hacienda House, a blonde blur at the door—but in the time it took this to register, the woman had disappeared. She leapt up to look: not a soul in the hall.

"I am worked up," she thought, "I am," seeing herself fast approaching the point where if someone so much as told her to take it easy she would explode. She could see how ridiculous it would be at this point, in this state, to call the police. But what she could do, had in fact long been meaning to do to protect her yard from the Luprestos' cur, was buy a BB gun, which she did after work; and this made her feel somewhat calmer.

The dog greeted her at the gate. Clutching her package, she said to the boys, who were standing nearby, on guard, "I've told you a million times, keep the dog out of the yard. He tramples the flowers."

Tommy looked at the yard, then back at her. "It's a dog," he said and climbed onto the motorbike; Billy got on behind him. "You can't tell him nothin. Freak!" The animal came shambling out and when they fired up the bike and rode away he loped along.

Inside, the telephone was ringing. After ten rings it stopped and Kay grabbed the phone book. She flipped through the pages until she found it, Johnson, D., and she dialed. There it was, that voice. Cradling the receiver, Kay noticed that the kitchen window, the one that looked out on the side yard, was missing its screen. When had that happened? She couldn't remember the last time she'd looked. Some guards—but had the boys gone to school? She'd forgotten about that, too.

She unwrapped the BB gun, the box of pellets, distracted herself for a minute with that, but then didn't know what to do. All evening she sat there, the phone ringing every half-hour, it seemed, until she looked down at her watch and couldn't see it in the dark and knew the calls had stopped.

There was a noise outside. A rustling, a subtle snap, it sounded loud in the kitchen, as if, without a screen, the window had let the outside in. All this while she had been sitting with the window open, but then, she thought, at least she wouldn't have to open it now. Creeping up on it, she raised the gun and, aiming at nothing, fired into the night. The suspense around her shattered with the shot. It hardly made a sound, a pop, but she felt the kick in her hand just as a howl rose in the yard.

A cry came at her, then something hurtling through the window, someone lighting on the sink, springing at her. Before she thought to raise her hands, she was falling, a battering weight on her, bellowing, "Bitch!"

"Tommy!" She heard the absurd note of recognition in her voice.

"You shot my brother!" he screamed at her. In a panic she struggled up, trying to ask if Billy was hurt, but Tommy sat on her. "Keep an eye out," he spat at her. The disgust seemed to wear him out, and he sat back, breathing short and shallow.

"Is he hurt?" she said, then saw beyond him the shadowy outline of Billy standing at the window. She fell back. "Get off of me," she said.

He didn't move. "Hey," Billy hissed, and Tommy slowly rose, dragging his toe on Kay's side as he stepped over her.

"You coulda blinded him," he said.

She started to say, "I thought it was the dog," but thought better of that. They were already gone, through the window, which she got up to close and lock as soon as her strength returned—and by then she had gotten past her panic over shooting a boy with a BB to wondering what he had been doing there in the first place, lurking around in her yard in the dark. Did they think they were guarding the house, with her in it? It was that woman, Kay thought, Dinah Johnson. If not for her, a person would know precisely what to make of two boys in her yard in the black night.

She lay in bed awake and tense, concentrated on the possibility of surprise, and when morning finally came she didn't know which was worse, staying home or leaving the house, which, after all, she decided was best, it was normal, it put her around people.

But then she had to face her students again, a battery of blank stares. They didn't want to be there either. So she gave them a test that took up the whole hour—an essay test, though, which was more work for her, too. Also, it allowed her to keep an eye on the door.

She was sitting alone in the lounge again in a near stupor, the warmth of the leaded sunlight working on her like a drug, when she heard her name. Instantly she was alert: the voice. And then, the silence. It was the waitress after all, a frowsy blonde with big blue eyes as hard and pale as glass, focused now on Kay, flat and coercive as her speech. Instead of the Mexican wedding dress she wore to serve, she was dressed in a suit and carried a large handbag. Kay glanced past her to see if anyone was passing, but the woman shifted, blocking the door. Still she stared, as if willing Kay to speak. Then she reached into her bag, and Kay said, "Oh my God."

The woman's hand froze for an instant. Slowly, watching Kay, she pulled a beer out of her purse and slowly, slowly, still watching, extended it. Kay was so relieved, she took it: warm. She popped the tab and, with the woman observing, took a sip. Then Dinah Johnson sat down.

"So," she said. They sat regarding one another for almost a minute before she went on, "Does it pay?"

"Pay?"

"Reviewing?"

"No."

"Oh. So." Another long pause passed. "How do you get into it?"

"Reviewing?" The woman nodded. "Just start doing it, I suppose."

"You suppose?"

"In my case, I mean."

"Just start? There's not some kind of food school?"

"I'm sure there is. But if you know your way around a meal and can write—."

"So I could do it?" She extracted another can of beer from her bag, pulled the tab, and took a swig, frowning. "But it doesn't pay." She shrugged. "You're right. Business is bad. But I get too much guff. It was the settlement in the divorce, my idea, I took the place, and Lee—the correspondent—he said I couldn't make it work or words to that effect. He always had to be right. Which is why I divorced him. There you go: right again." She got up, tipped back her beer. "I'm selling," she said. "What I need is a week or two at Cardinal."

Kay just looked up at her, not knowing what to say and feeling too drained to say anything anyway. The can of beer was heavy in her hand. "Good luck," she finally ventured, but she wasn't satisfied. The moment seemed to merit more—Dinah Johnson, too, whose frustration she thought she could understand, especially after the menace of the past few days, which had accrued to her like so much more "guff."

"Right," the woman said, a weary word, then turned to go, and Kay called out, "Wait!" She wasn't thinking. "Can I—" she said, but then couldn't come up with anything that she might do. Dinah Johnson was waiting. "We could have dinner," Kay said and was suddenly embarrassed.

The woman continued to look at her. "Two food experts," she finally remarked. "It's three o'clock."

"That's right." Kay remembered her house now, left in the keeping of those two hoodlums. "I could make something," she said. "Nothing fancy, but—" she shrugged, although she wasn't feeling nonchalant, was in fact feeling more hurried by the moment.

After some consideration, Dinah Johnson said, "I got nothing better to do."

As if she'd made a keen tactical move, Kay was pleased almost to the point of agitation to lead the woman to her car. Dinah Johnson made a face at the classical music on the radio and turned it off. With the same skeptical expression, she appraised Kay's neighborhood and then her house, and then went in and made herself at home on the sofa with a magazine. "*Country Life?*" she said, as if it were a conundrum.

Looking through the cupboards and then in the refrigerator, Kay felt embarrassed again. "There's no food here," she said, "I didn't realize," and Dinah Johnson came into the kitchen.

"Graham crackers," the woman said, making an inspection. "Powdered milk. A box of raisins, unopened, I see. Two eggs and some unknown juice."

"That's the lot," Kay admitted. "Oh, lettuce in the drawer."

"Wouldn't want to forget that," Dinah Johnson said. She was exercising her frown on the cupboard. "I can make some kind of pancake out of graham crackers. I been meaning to try it."

"You have?" Kay tried to look encouraging. What did she know about graham-cracker pancakes?

Just then the doorbell rang and Lou came in, already exclaiming, "Where have you been? I tried calling all night."

"Dinah Johnson," Kay said. "This is Lou."

"Dinah Johnson?" At once his demeanor changed. If he were a dog, Kay was thinking, his tail would be wagging. "Kay's told me a bit about your situation," he said, and though this surprised Kay somewhat it seemed to please Dinah.

"It's a sad story," she said.

Lou told her that he would be happy to listen, if she wanted to talk about it, and Dinah was leading him into the living room, where, she said, they would be more comfortable; "Like I told your friend," she was saying, when the bell rang again and Kay went to the door to find Tommy and Billy standing on the step. Behind her she could hear Dinah humming along, Lou's occasional soft undertone.

"You said come back later," Tommy said with a smirk. "Here we are."

"There's no more work for you here," Kay said. "And there

never will be. Furthermore, if you set foot in my yard again, I'll shoot you. That goes for your dog, too. If I *hear* that you've been anywhere near my house, I'll shoot you. In fact, if I see you again I might shoot you, just on principle. So you'd better get going. Now."

Tommy sank a bit into his shoulders and shifted. "Hey," he said to his brother, "see anything funny? a *strange woman,* like?"

Billy had already started away, but he managed to answer, "Ha-ha," as they both slunk off, casting looks back at her over their shoulders.

"Kay!" Lou exclaimed. She turned to find him standing in the doorway to the living room, Dinah behind him.

"You got style," Dinah said. "Either that, or a problem. But I can relate."

"Kay!" Lou said again. "How could you—."

"Oh, Lou, why don't you go, too?" she said, feeling strangely exhilarated.

"I—."

"If you hurry, you can catch the boys. Maybe they're ready for counseling now."

"Kay!" He stood staring at her while she held the door open. When she didn't move, he finally started out, pausing on the step to say her name again, a question, then watching her all the way down the walk, much as the twins had. "I'll call you," he said uncertainly, and she closed the door.

"A nice guy," Dinah said. "Very therapeutic. I feel better already."

Kay said, "So do I."

"You know, it's getting to where I should open the restaurant," Dinah said, glancing at the box of graham crackers sitting on the kitchen table. "Since I didn't shut it down yet. It's tamale night."

"Tamale night?"

"Cold today, hot tamale. I bet you never reviewed the tamales."

"No," Kay said, "I didn't."

"That was your mistake," Dinah told her, opening the door. "Stick with me. You might learn something about restaurants yet."

Kay stood there casting around, finally focusing on her purse. I got nothing better to do, she heard herself think, just as the woman had said it. But what she said, as Dinah Johnson let her out of her own house, was, "If you say so. But I'm not reviewing anymore."

"If you say so," Dinah Johnson said.

3 A.M., Your Father

"You don't have to say anything."
"But let me."
"No. I heard enough tonight."
"I know. Let me explain."
"Explain what? You don't know. I fell in love with him."
"I don't believe it, and I don't believe you do, either."
"I did."
"You think that makes it easier?"
"No. It makes it harder."
"Oh, self-pity. That's easy enough."
"What did he tell you? Did he tell you I seduced him?"
"No."
"He didn't?"
"No."
"I did. But I didn't know what I was doing."
"Honey, I give you more credit than that."
"I didn't know the *extent*. This was three years ago. You don't know what he was like."
"Three years."
"I was shopping. I just . . . met him. I got interested."
"He was—on display?"
"He was working. At Robertson's."
"A salesclerk."
"So? He was only fifteen."
"And you were what? But that didn't occur to you. Because you were in love. Oh, all right, you weren't in love, yet. Just shopping at this point."
"Are you having fun?"
"No. I don't enjoy hearing you call a hankering for something at Robertson's love."
"Oh, am I supposed to entertain you? What would you enjoy? Just the hankering—that's more your style. It wasn't that, and yes, I noticed, but it didn't matter. It wasn't an issue. Because he was attractive, like any man who's attractive, except more."
"You forget I know the boy."
"You didn't know him then."

"That makes a difference?"

"Yes. I'm trying to tell you. It didn't seem like anything. I kept going back there, pretending I was looking for a ribbon (he worked in notions; I said I was trying to match a dress). And he kept waiting on me. I thought it was a regular flirtation."

"Regular? With one party wearing diapers?"

"*Two-sided.*"

"Ah. You were flirting. He was salesclerking."

"How long can a person look for one stupid ribbon? I thought he was playing along. He looked like he was."

"Now wait."

"No, he had that look—you know what I mean—it makes you think someone knows everything."

"My generation calls it a leer."

"No, it's nice. It's . . . appreciative. And that's how Jim looked. But that was just the way he looked. That was Jim. He thought there was a dress."

"So why didn't you leave him alone?"

"I told you, I didn't know. He said bring the dress in—'Maybe you should bring the dress in and save yourself some trouble,' and I thought—I said he should come over and see it for himself."

"And he said, 'I'm sorry, Miss, that's not my job.' "

"He came over."

"And you expect me to believe he didn't know what you were up to?"

"I don't think he did. Until he had to."

"Kate, I know fifteen. What was the boy? Retarded?"

"Innocent."

"Do you know why I came over here?"

"To gloat."

"Gloat, my God, the opposite. I was thinking of your mother."

"I'm not like her."

"You proved it, didn't you?"

"I wasn't proving anything. I fell in love with him."

"I remember. I didn't believe it."

"You can't stand it, can you? I fell in love with someone half my age. I sat right here and waited for him. When I thought about him, I could feel my pulse—here and here and—."

"A minute ago he was innocent."

"I took care of that."

"Now we're getting there."

"We've been there. That's what I was telling you. Maybe he had an inkling. But when it really dawned on him, I could tell. I could see it. And I could have stopped it. But there was something nice about him."

"You're right. I can't stand it. Let me tell you something."

"So I didn't. Stop it."

"It concerns your uncle. It has a moral."

"So does this."

"I'm afraid I know it."

"You can't. You didn't know him. When he figured out what he was doing here, I could tell, and I could tell because he looked—concerned. Do you know what I mean? He didn't want to let me know he'd just figured it out."

"No. That would be embarrassing."

"For me. That's what I mean."

"That was his 'concern'? Is that what you're saying?"

"Yes."

"One look, three years ago. Your memory's embellishing."

"My memory's fine. Why do you think I went ahead?"

"Don't ask me to answer that. You said you didn't know what you were doing."

"The *extent.*"

"I know what you're getting at, Katie, people change, especially fifteen year-olds."

"I ruined him."

"Ruined. So dramatic."

"It is. He's a man now and look at him."

"I have. He's a boy. A good boy."

"Oh! You admired the way he told you he was screwing your daughter. It took a good boy to do that."

"Kate."

"You had to run over at three in the morning to tell me what a good boy—."

"You don't understand."

"Yes I do. What did he say? I don't care. This is what happened. He came over here—he woke me up. Before I turned on the light outside I couldn't tell who it was. Then he said, 'Come *on,*' and I said, 'Wake up, Kate, it's just Jim.'

"I told him go home, I was sleeping. He said no. No. Just Jim, all right, wake up, Kate. I said, 'No?' And he pushed me out of the way. He's bigger than me—he didn't used to be—and I never thought about that. But he did.

"He was sitting in the kitchen, his favorite spot. I turned on the light—and there was that bruise, and I thought, God, he's hurt, that's why all this. His eye was bleeding. I went—and he knocked me away. So hard, he knocked over his chair and I had to grab the counter to stay up. Then he picked up his chair and sat down and didn't say anything. I asked him what happened. He said, 'Nothing.' I said, 'Come on, *something* happened.'

" 'Nothing happened.' "

"Nothing?"

"He wouldn't tell me."

"He wouldn't?"

"No, why? He told you?"

"No. He didn't tell me."

"He wouldn't say anything. He just sat there. I told him to go home. I told him his mother'd be worried—and I wasn't being sarcastic. You know what he said? 'She thinks I'm having an affair. She thinks it's good for me.' Then he smiled.

"I'm a coward. I said, 'Let's go to bed.' But he didn't move. So I said, 'Jim, I'm tired.' He said, 'Then go to bed.'

"So I did. I said I'm a coward. I thought: in the morning, everything'll be fine. And I'll do something."

"And here we are. Morning."

"Yeah, and everything's fine."

"It could be worse."

"I hit him. He came and sat next to the bed like some kind of guard dog. I couldn't sleep with him sitting there staring at me. I tried talking to him, but—I pretended to sleep. Then I was having a nightmare and Jim was shaking me. He was in the nightmare like that, shaking me. So I hit him. But I was awake. He went back to his chair and sat there just like before. When I woke up again he was gone."

"He won't bother you anymore. Don't you dare start to cry. You wanted to be rid of him—isn't that the gist of this?"

"No."

"Now that he's 'ruined' he's not much fun?"

"No."

"No, that's right. Let's not cry for *Jim.* Now will you be quiet while I tell you? Your moral's lost on me. At least mine's comforting."

"What good's a moral coming from you?"

"Not much, apparently. I raised you wrong."

"You didn't raise me."

"If I had, you wouldn't've made that remark. You think morals are only as good as the people who say them?"

"Yes."

"Stop being contrary. You're wasting my time."

"*I'm* wasting *your* time?"

"Yes, my time's precious. I'm an antique."

"Then why don't you go home. Jenny can oil you. Jenny, right?"

"Jenny, right. Jenny will be there. Who's caring for you? I wouldn't dismiss me so fast. Don't start that again, here, I'm sorry—listen to me. You admire your uncle."

"I don't know him."

"Oh come on, Kate, I was there for a while. I heard your mother nominate him for sainthood a number of times. You know him well enough."

"No I don't."

"He's that rare and wonderful thing, a virtuous man. Owen the virtuous. When a daughter of Owen's shops, she buys ribbons."

"I should've known—."

"Better. You should've known better. But as you can see, I'm not absolving myself. *Now* that you know Owen as well as any woman in her right mind would want to—no, that's a lie. I admire my brother, I always have, and if I were a woman—but that's beside the point."

"What *is* the point?"

"I'm getting to that. Don't be impatient. Saint Owen at seventeen had an affair—it boggles the mind—with a woman quite close to your age. There. You see the connection. But she wasn't like you. She didn't have the appearance of respectability. And I don't think love was what she was after with Owen, though she probably would have said love to him—he'd want to hear it, you know.

"Granted, I'm guessing a little. But I saw her—Penny, appropriate name—and even though I was only knee-high at the time, I was plenty old enough to form an opinion. Owen took me past her house one day when he was supposed to be watching me. I was the baby. I had to be watched. He said we weren't going anywhere, but not going anywhere we somehow got to a very strange place—strange to me—run-down houses, no trees, patchy yards—each with its fence. And out came a woman. She was wearing a robe, not much of a robe, a goddess, I gasped, she was waiting for us. Owen, rather. She put a hand on each side of his face and pulled him up against her with the fence in between them. Whatever she was doing, Owen got jumpy. He said, 'Shit, Penny,' and reached for me. I'd never heard 'shit' from my brother before. I was impressed.

"This was our secret, then: Penny. You see how it had to be. And I was proud of that. I knew where Owen was when he went 'nowhere' and nobody else did. It made him more mine. So, I knew it went on, it went on for some time, but that's not the point."

"What is?"

"The end. I'm getting to that. But first there's your aunt and a young man named Michael. Becky was young once, it seems hard to believe, but take my word for it. Young as she was, sixteen, I'd say, she'd ruined scads of boys—that's what she said anyway. You see, the word 'ruin'?—it's diluted for me. If Becky at sixteen could use it to boast. . . . At the time, she was seeing a sweet college boy—this Michael. He was funny and shy and I liked him immensely. I remember his hands, how they moved—awkward amounting to graceful. Don't be impatient. I want you to know that Michael was delicate. Becky, to be sure, hadn't mentioned those scads to him.

"The crux of it, then. I was spying on them, Becky and Michael, from the living-room door, and I was getting what you might call an eyeful. Beck was voluptuous, you can't imagine, and I'd say she wanted Michael to appreciate this. He was having a difficult time of it—so obviously smitten, so clearly concerned, yes, concerned, about the . . . propriety? Comical, isn't it? He was frustrating her with his respect. But that can't last forever—I said he was smitten—and it didn't. Becky had her way.

"And who should walk in on this charming scene but Owen, just home from nowhere, carrying his shoes, Kate. I didn't know he was there till he dropped them. He'd come in through the kitchen and I couldn't see him—it was dark, I forgot that, it must be important. We were all supposed to be snug in our beds: me, Becky, Owen.

"Let me back up a bit. What does Owen see as he comes up the walk? Michael's bike. A crooked old thing, missing some spokes. Owen looks at this bike and he takes off his shoes and creeps into the house. I'm making this up—not the bike; it was real—Owen's entrance.

"But, thud, there he was, also real. They scrambled, but Owen was fast. He got to the sofa before they were off of it and wrenched Becky up by the arm. She didn't make a sound. She was too smart for that. And Owen was silent. Everyone was aware of the parents asleep—and me, too, they thought.

"Michael's reaction was classic. He was—let's call it dishevelled—but he seemed to forget that. Without a single straightening fumble for himself, he tried to come between Becky and Owen. But Owen was trying to get between Michael and Becky, so we had a tug of war with Becky in the middle, hissing something inane at Owen, 'Mind your own business,' something like that, and Owen hissing at Michael, 'Get out.' He kept pushing him away and saying, 'Get out,' and finally Michael did. He had to. Owen had the advantage of size—and righteousness, as Michael probably saw it.

"But, then. Becky fell back on the sofa and lay there and glared up at Owen, glared. I couldn't see his face. He didn't say anything for a second. Then he said—and I think it sounded more violent than it was because of the whisper—he said, 'Leave him alone. And if you try anything on that kid again—.' He didn't finish. He cursed and turned around and picked up his shoes. When he unbent he saw me—in my enthusiasm, I'd got reckless—but I might not've been there. He might've been staring into a hole, for a second, and then he went out.

"By then, Becky'd seen me, too, of course. As soon as Owen left, she threatened me with my life and sent me to bed. Where I stayed awake waiting for Owen's return—a few hours, I guess, a few eternities by eight-year-old time. What do you think?"

"I think you're making this up."

"God, no. I treasured these things in my heart. I knew they'd serve me some day. No, wait, here's the thing. Owen went to Penny, I'm certain of that. There was no more sneaking out after that, no more aimless walking that led to one place, no more Penny, I knew it, I mourned her, our secret—all gone. And no more Michael, either, for Becky, at least, though I'm sure he lived on and no doubt became an Elk or a Mason or a Knight of Columbus right beside Owen. Everyone got what was best—or what he deserved, anyway—even me, now that I think of it. There's a fairness to these things."

"Fairness. Is that it? The moral?"

"Maybe not a moral. It illustrates something."

"What? You think Jim went through something like that? We're out of the Dark Ages."

"Some of us are. Do you even see what I'm saying? It doesn't have to be algebraic. Whatever Michael prompted in Owen was there all along, it still is; it just needed a jog, it needed a Michael. But it didn't have to be *Michael.* Your Jim caught up with himself tonight, that's all."

"That wasn't *my* Jim. That wasn't Jim 'all along.' "

"Three years older—what did you expect?"

"I expected him to stay nice."

"*Nice.* He is nice. You didn't expect his seriousness. You didn't count on that in a boy. And you say you didn't know what you were doing. God help me, I believe you. Else how could you keep on? How could you think that what got you into this thing in the first place would just go away?"

"I didn't—I couldn't—take it seriously."

"There. And he couldn't take that."

"He took it. He had to keep up."

"Why should he? Have to? You're proving my point."

"No I'm not. He *kept up* by turning into someone who wouldn't've interested me. In the first place. You forgot tonight."

"I'm remembering it. Every word, every detail."

"You don't know it all. Don't you want to know how he found you?"

"I'm not sure I do."

"That night you met him? He followed you home."

"He told you that?"

"Not till tonight. He said he was jealous. He *knew* you were my *father,* I told him—you don't even remember. You were drunk."

"Drunk was not what I was. I remember vividly, such a pretty picture. A brutish boy of seventeen sitting on my daughter's doorstep, waiting to be babysat. You think I'd forget that?"

"He wasn't brutish."

"Babysitting. An indication of the sort of fool you take me for."

"So you remember. He didn't believe me."

"He told you that tonight."

"After I told him to leave me alone, for good—but I didn't say it like that. I tried to be nice. I told you I tried—talking to him. I knew it wasn't going to be all right in the morning. At the rate we were going, it'd be morning in a minute and he'd still be sitting there staring at me. So I tried. But he said no. So I said I wouldn't see him anymore. He said I had to. Had to. I didn't know what to say, I don't even remember what I said, 'I won't,' something, just words. He said, 'I'll tell your father.' He meant it. It was supposed to be a threat. So it was, just that he said it, and I just kept talking, to say anything. I said 'You couldn't find him. We have different names'—I know how it sounds, but I was trying to think what to do. Then he smiled like that again and said, '1020 Maple? Alex Cavanaugh, man of the world?' "

"Oh Lord."

"Then he told me he followed you. That was it. I told him, 'Go ahead. Tell him. I don't care.' He just looked at me. Like he didn't believe it. So I said, 'I don't. And my Dad won't either.' "

"*Enough.*"

"That's not all."

"No it's not. That boy didn't tell me a word of this mess. Don't look at me that way. I can't match the grand gesture of an idiot eighteen-year-old, but I can advertise it. Followed me home? You're twice the idiot he is. *I* followed *him.* What kind of doddering father do you think I am? I knew what I was up to at his age, and babysitting wasn't what we called it. And any man with half a mind would've recognized the exquisite relief in his face when you said, 'Meet my father.' Even with my half a mind I did, and I waited till the little brute left, and I dogged him. We talked man to man, ha-ha, this was my part: Stay away from my daughter. This was his part: No. You see, I've experienced Jim's obstinance. So I tacked. I played *his* father, whose part I didn't even know, and I told him what was good for him and what most definitely was not.

"He was stubborn. We've been regular buddies for the past year, Jimmers and me. I talk about responsibility, a new suit of mine, what a fit, and Jim? Jim talks about love. Oh love, the soft coin of adolescence."

"You shit."

"Wait. I'm getting to the good part. Tonight. A very small thing, yes, the straw—Jenny is capable of having a brother Jim's age, and tonight we had his unpleasant company forced on us. There's your leer, it still lives, a more unpleasant boy you can't—on our release, I went straight to where Jim works and waited. Quite a step up from notions. I waited and when he came out I told him that since he insisted on talking about love, we would. I told him the obvious. You weren't in love with him. You never would be. You never were. I told him he only had you at all because you *couldn't* be.

"*Don't interrupt me.* There's that look. You learned that from him. That's how he looked—before he took a swing at me. That's right. You would've thought he was on your side, not me. He's a prince. A *prince,* Jim the Chivalrous, but paternal love is bigger than all that.

"I flattened him. *That* is where that bruise came from. And *that* is what happened."

"You—."

"Wait."

"You set it up."

"*No.* I didn't know. One minute later, I thought I'd done the opposite of what I thought I was doing. But I came here anyway. I came to hear it."

"And you did, didn't you? You sat here and let me tell you—."

"I didn't want to, I didn't, and I didn't mean to—but once you got started, once I did, I thought . . . for a minute I thought I'd come through unscathed."

"You. Jim."

"Yes. Jim."

"That's why you hit him. Your stupid pride."

"Stupid pride . . . I blackened the eye of a boy young enough to be my grandson."

"Because he was right and he wouldn't back down. You humiliated him. So he came over mad. And look—."

"Look."

"I don't have to. It's so obvious."

"*Look.* He came over here. *And what?*"

"Now he thinks—"

"Knows."

"Thinks, because you—"

"—were right."

"That's all you care about."

"Asinine girl, I care about you. Why do you think I harassed him?"

"Because he was easy—"

"Easy, my God."

"—and you couldn't face me."

"Okay, I couldn't, think about that—why not? Your fearsome polemics? I'm sorry, no; I'm not sorry. Then, what? Shame for my daughter the vamp? I don't think so. This would look like kindergarten on my resumé. Preschool. So why?"

"*Why?*"

"I told you I thought of your mother. And I did, way back then, your mother and me. What we did to you."

"Oh right."

"Yes, right."

"I was fine till—."

"Fine, maybe, but you don't know it. Or you wouldn't be frittering yourself away on a boy just because he isn't old enough to know the harm he can do."

"So now he knows."

"That's not the point."

"What is? Why *did* you harass him? Why'd you hit him? You

had to tell me that stupid story. Okay. What's the point? Everyone has a part, isn't that it? I'm supposed to be Penny, great. What about Jim? He's supposed to be Owen, isn't he? Wasn't that it? But what about when he was sweet? What about Michael, you liked him so much. And if he was so good, he didn't need help—you said that, too. Owen was just showing off. He was helping himself. What's the point of the story, Dad? What part do you play?"

"I tell the story. I don't play at all."

"Owen. You admire him, I don't. You think you saved someone."

"*All right.* I was trying to help. I could see. *I* could feel your pulse, and it made me sick. I didn't even dope it out that night. I was just sick, so I got hold of Jim and I hemmed and I hawed—and if you think my earlier performance was something. You thought I was drunk. This would have mortified you. No *wonder* he wouldn't listen.

"Then I thought—I mean, why should this bother me, I—but I thought. This is what it came to. I thought: this, this business with a boy, this is her—yes, your—way of avoiding me, not just me, your mother, too. No, not literally. You know what I mean. Our brilliant examples. My kind isn't obsolete. And if your *mother* was susceptible, there's one of me for you, too. That never occurred to me, that you might think that; there's some of me in you, so it seemed absurd. I did give you something, besides nothing. But then it obsessed me.

"And your mother—oh I know, you're not like her, you say it so fast. If you believed it, would you devote three years to someone you 'couldn't take seriously?'—I'm in the past, the past tense: I *thought.* Thought. And I thought: so, it catches up. My fecklessness. In the one person in the world I had to love.

"Why couldn't I face you. You weren't far wrong when you said easy—you see why I couldn't, thinking that way. But I thought I'd do something. I'd make it go away without letting you catch the faintest whiff of what was in my mind, you see where you got your cowardice—but I was *protecting* you. Sad, isn't it, what a taste of righteousness can do to a man, coming when he's near an age where he won't be good for much else. Screws up the judgment, doesn't it, Kate?"

"It's pathetic."

"Not yet, Kate. Not at first. At first—everything would be all right in the morning, you know—maybe that's good for a minute, or a night, maybe another one. But not for a year. I bored myself. I said the same things again and again. Till I made *myself* sick, the sound of my voice—which was harder and harder to believe, and tonight. Tonight, that oily brother of Jenny's. I looked and I listened and I knew what it was. It wasn't my voice; it was Jim's. *He'd* convinced *me.* Not innocence. The opposite. His knowing. He was absolutely sure of you. And I was vain. What was I doing? Not any good. Nothing. I wasn't a threat to you. I wasn't anything.

"I could have despised Jim for that. Easy. But my God I envied him."

"Pathetic."

"Yes. Now's the time. Now I despise him—for being such a fool. You *are* all right, aren't you, Kate? You fooled everyone."

"I was in love with him."

"And what the hell difference does that make? You keep saying so. It's not a charm. Love's easy."

"Hard."

"You never got that far."

"Oh, and you have."

"If you don't know it by now, then I think so. Yes, I think so. I have."

The Easy Version

The piano teacher had the long hands and the long face and the eyes that were no color. But more in attitude than features he was the spitting image of her brother who'd died in the Peace Corps after doing good for nine months and two weeks. He had the knowing look her brother might have had if he'd been allowed to live longer, along with a worldly ease that some people associated with manliness but May saw as a surface and a sign, still water. She took the man's long hand and in her mind made a note not to say certain things to him.

She wouldn't say, "Six of one, half a dozen of the other" or "How do you like them apples?" or any other hand-me-down expressions from her mother, who was a simple woman with simple expressions. She wouldn't say, "Now you're cooking with gas," which she'd picked up as far back as fourth grade. Her piano teacher then, Mrs. Gooding, had used this remark for approval and had shown May pictures taken when she'd sung opera and her short white hair was red and reached the bottom of her back. The pictures came from a time when "Now you're cooking with gas" was a meaningful saying; but a woman of May's generation couldn't say it with meaning, and it was crude, now that she thought about it. Also, she would have to decide about "piano teacher" in reference to Leslie Swanson. It sounded fine from a fourth grader, but too girlish for someone her age, though "pianist" gave her trouble and didn't have the teacher in it.

Leslie Howard was the only other man May knew of named Leslie, and, even though he was a big name in *Gone with the Wind,* he wasn't exactly altogether there, as the movie proved, and as any man might falter under the name Leslie—at least she'd thought so until she'd met the pianist. When Leslie Swanson wasn't all there, he seemed to be somewhere better.

When she copied his fingering for the scales and he gave her a look meant for a prodigy, she couldn't tell him about Mrs. Gooding and the fourth through eighth grades. That he could give her more than just the C scale seemed to bring some of him out of wherever his mind was. She had to ask him twice not to call her Mrs. Greene.

He said, "I like to preserve formalities, out of respect for my students."

" 'Mrs. Greene' doesn't mean respect," she said, "except for Mr. Greene."

Leslie Swanson wouldn't want to pay that small respect to Mr. Greene if he knew how little respect Mr. Greene would pay back, saying piano lessons were a foolish notion, as he'd said about ballet lessons and French and anything else she did to better herself, even though she was the one to ask when a country singer put a French phrase between children and divorce. It was what she got for marrying at nineteen when she couldn't tell that knowing Mr. Greene at thirty-five was knowing him at fifty-one.

That was the cause of the only fight she'd ever had with her brother, and that fight went on from the day she'd announced her engagement until the day she'd made good on it. He said she was settling for something with Mr. Greene. He said Mr. Greene would hold her back. She said, "From what?" and he looked away, as he did when he was looking inward, and then he might say, "What you've got to do," or maybe, "Something better," but he never explained. So she had her way in their one and only fight and stuck it out with Mr. Greene and never knew whether his being Mr. Greene from first to last was the reason for her sticking it out or the reason for her twinges, which she wouldn't call self-pity; they were just her way of remembering that there was something better she was supposed to know about.

With Leslie Swanson, she had to wonder, too. He had a way of explaining, dropping silent while he waited for a word they could both use, that made her sure of a world right next to her full of words he could hear but she couldn't, the way a dog heard whistles people didn't. It was in those times of no talking, when she was straining to get what wasn't being said, that she sometimes got frustrated and wondered what was the point of listening if everything she could hear had to be said on a level where she already was. But Leslie Swanson smiled before he came out with his explanations, and she got that good feeling that just knowing something was in there where the words weren't was enough.

After her lesson he played some of the number Beethoven wrote stone deaf and she sighed. He said, "You don't like this piece?"

And she said, "It reminds me life is full of sorrow."

"That it is," he said, "and every day I thank God that we have music to remind us."

"What I meant," she said, "is all you get is what he got out of his head and put on paper." Maybe, being a genius, Beethoven thought other people could figure out sadness just from hearing it.

May told Mr. Greene that he'd been too quick to judge and that piano lessons were a fine idea she'd had and would have her giving an inspired performance for him before he could say Jack Sprat.

He said, "Jack Sprat."

She said, "What could I expect from someone who thinks Elvis is one of the greats?"

He said, "You know what to expect," and put a Lou Rawls record on.

"There's nothing like a live performance," she said.

He said, "Right."

All that time they'd had the upright from her mother's house in the living room with no one knowing how to play anything but the easy versions of "Ode to Joy" and "The Rite of Spring." She hadn't known it was the easy version until she'd played the Rite for Joe Mulligan. That was the night she found out from Kate Mulligan about the pianist Kate went to to keep up. She wasn't going to play anymore for someone to tell her it was the easy version, and she had her own money from working at the D.M.V. to pay for whatever kind of notions she wanted.

The next week May saw the student whose half-hour came before hers, Miss Gracie, Leslie called her, even though she couldn't be more than fourteen years old. May spotted her at once for a girl precocious enough to know she hadn't bloomed yet but pushing to bloom early anyway, with the dress and shoes just like updated copies of what she herself had thought was smart twenty years ago, and the same blue eye shadow on droopy lids, which passed for worldliness.

"You met Miss Gracie," Leslie said when she took her seat on the piano bench.

"I wouldn't say met," May said.

"She wasn't rude?" he said, as if she could be.

"On, no." She laid a protesting touch on his hand where it curved up from the wood below the keyboard, with one finger tapping a note but not making a sound. "Just wrapped up in being young and promising."

He waited till she took her hand away, then slowly moved his own to open the exercise book and smiled to himself. When she played the scales and finger exercises, he complimented her on her quick learning and asked her how she happened to be so dexterous. "The I.B.M.," she said and typed the air. "That Miss Gracie must be all of thirteen, despite the 'Miss.' "

"Sixteen," he said, then smiled at himself for being so quick to correct. "At that age every year's crucial, you know."

May asked, "Is she gifted?" and he said, "Oh, very."

In the middle of the week, she met Kate Mulligan for lunch and thanked her for the tip on Leslie Swanson. She was glad to be learning piano from a man with some depth, she said.

Kate laughed her laugh. "You'd be surprised," she said. "At the bottom of everything deep is dirt."

May was hurt because they'd said her brother was deep before he died, and it was her highest compliment to Leslie Swanson. "Tragedy is deep," she said.

Kate said, "Well I never saw a tragedy without some dirt."

May said, "Maybe it's in your eyes."

Kate made a big-eyed face and laughed, as if it didn't matter much whether what she saw was in her way of seeing or out in the world.

Before her lesson May put Mr. Greene's favorite meal into the oven, beef roast rolled in garlic and baked potatoes. He complained about the garlic, said it worked on him in mysterious ways, but he always wanted the end piece, where the most garlic was. That was the way Mr. Greene would talk, just to say what he didn't mean because he didn't consider appreciation a masculine virtue unless it came in the form of a complaint.

Every day when she practiced he turned down the record or TV even though he rolled his eyes on each stroll past the piano, more out of habit than sincerity. She wanted him to have his favorite dinner because it had occurred to her the day before how dry his life was with everything a habit or a foolish notion.

She tied back her hair so her cheekbones would be in full view, and brushed some blush on them. Her face with a touch of blush looked like a face that had been outside enjoying the weather instead of bending over vehicle registration forms and getting fumes from the Vanish and Spic'n'Span and garlic. Her hands were another story, but dexterous. She guessed that she was three or four years younger than Leslie Swanson, who must be thirty-eight or thirty-nine, and what a lonely life.

Something she couldn't recognize except for its excellence was being played on the piano when she got to the door of Leslie's apartment. She looked at the crack that ran down one wall, under the hall carpet and up the other side, and thought about how she wasn't even almost old and already there were babies like Miss Gracie growing up in the world. Then the girl came out, dressed in blue jeans and a T-shirt, just a little mascara and smudgy lip gloss, like a girl properly sixteen years old.

Leslie was standing between the bench and the piano. "That is one gifted child," May said as she sat down next to him. Looking surprised, he sat down, too, so close that she could feel the hairs on their arms touching, so all she had to do to make the contact skin was shift as if she didn't mean it.

He said, "What do you mean?"

She said, "I heard that playing and I know I was impressed."

He said, "Thank you," which seemed like an odd thing to say, but at second thought okay, because what was the accident of talent without a teacher to make it a sure thing?

Again he got out the exercises, and she said, "I don't know why I can't start on a piece if I'm so dexterous."

"A piece?" he said. "All right," and produced a Chopin prelude that she couldn't even play one hand of, let alone two.

"That's a good one," she said. "Why not the deaf Beethoven while I'm at it?"

"You can't be impatient. You have to master the fundamentals first." He said it with resignation, as if the fundamentals were as tedious for him as they were for her. She told him that there must be something easier for a beginner not to get bored. There were abridgments, he admitted, and turned to the easy version of "Ode to Joy" in Thompson. "If you insist," he said, "but I still say you're forcing the process."

"I thought you weren't going to play that anymore," her husband said.

She said, "Begin at the beginning."

"Stay at the beginning is more like it." He made a thunk by

pressing his finger on the lowest A and said, "I don't trust a man who gives piano lessons to Kate Mulligan."

"And what does that mean?"

"Don't tell me you haven't heard as much about her as I have, and probably from the horse's mouth." She didn't say. "And when did you ever hear her play a note?" He assumed from her silence that she had difficulty answering, so he said, "That's right, never. And that's when you'll hear it, too."

He liked a conversation that ended on 'never.' That was his way of getting into what she was doing and staying there as a mental note. Sometimes she thought it was funny and sometimes she didn't, but this time she kept playing and thought about Kate's laugh, which embarrassed everyone except Kate but was balanced out by the fact that she laughed at everyone's jokes, even the sorriest attempts; and men liked that and the way she threw her head back laughing and made a person think of passion. Joe said that Kate was manic-depressive because she had her periods of being adventurous and her periods of being sorry for it. May was remembering her dirt remark. She pressed on the blur pedal so the notes wouldn't be too jarring by themselves.

"Hmmm," Leslie said and took her foot off the pedal by hooking her ankle with the toe of his shoe. Then he let her foot go and returned to the place where he'd been deep down for ten minutes.

"What about Kate Mulligan?" she said. "Is she gifted?"

He said, "Hmmm."

"Everybody is gifted," she said. "And what about Miss Gracie? No lesson today?" For a second she was sorry for giving him a start when he was thinking.

"No," he said, "she's gone beyond my modest talents." She gave some thought to his tone, which was no compliment to the girl's progress. He went into one of his silences and then came out with, "I don't think it's a good policy to discuss one student with another," which was simpler than whatever he'd been thinking for so long. So much like her brother, his way of letting a person know the difference, it gave her the ghost. She wondered whether she'd been spooked or had really heard a noise in the next room, which was closed and so didn't give a clue. "I'm sorry," she said and looked at her fingers and counted to ten. "Do you have a cat?"

"A cat?"

Un chat, she thought. "I thought I heard a noise," she said and nodded at the door.

"That's funny." He looked at her like someone who was afraid of prowlers but would rather wait for them than go see and be sure; so she stood up. Before she took a step, Leslie stopped her with a long hand on either side of her face and said, "Perhaps you heard the piano not making any noise." That was a long time to have his hands on her face. She could feel another blush under the one she'd put on.

"What kind of student am I?" she said, taking his hands away and laughing, not like Kate, but embarrassing just the same.

"Fast," he answered. "Your mastery of a moment ago was a nice surprise."

"I didn't think you noticed."

"I know you didn't." Then he was tugging on her hand so she'd sit down, and she was thinking gratefully of the ballet lessons, which had given her the grace to sit down so well even if she was almost losing her balance. She had to reach over him every time she went down the scales, a difficult maneuver because he was sitting so close, making her think.

Then he tried to give her something called "Melody" from Mozart's Sonata in A; but she thought about following her performance of "Ode to Joy" with a flub of a simple thing like melody and thumbed through the book until she could pretend to be struck by "The Rite of Spring." Along with that assignment, she told herself she'd have to work on "Melody" and get it to where she could accept it as homework next week and still keep up with herself. Before going, she stopped to look at the painting hanging on the wall next to the closed room. It was a white square with black lines that could be bare trees or TV antennas. Leslie was standing at the door, waiting. "Next week, then," he said.

She was still standing in the hall with the crack running under her, wondering how she could have Mrs. Gooding's lessons at her fingertips without Leslie Swanson guessing that she wasn't learning everything from him, especially since he was so big on the fundamentals, when a door slammed inside the apartment and Leslie started speaking.

She could only recognize the tone, which had the question mark she'd heard in other men's voices when they already had their answers. Then a girl said, "Oh, come off it," and May thought: If I hear anymore, it'd have to be because I wanted to.

She was halfway down the stairs when the door above her

opened and shut and Miss Gracie came down. The girl brushed past and went out to stand on the curb that Leslie Swanson's living room had a view of. After a few seconds of touching the street with the toe of one sneaker, she twisted around and gave May a look.

May said, "Miss Gracie?"

"Don't call me that." She turned back to the street and said, "It wasn't my idea to hide. What a sap." When she turned around again, her face was halfway made up to be cynical. She said, "Everybody said he had to have something wrong with him to go for me. Just because I'm fourteen."

May tried not to think about Leslie's fib while she looked for an answer for the girl. The hard part was not knowing why Miss Gracie would say what she'd said to someone she hadn't even had a hello for until now. May said, "Everybody is too many people to be in agreement and be trusted."

"Oh, you don't know," the girl said. "Everybody was right." Then she stepped into the street and started walking away, kicking the side of her foot against the curb as she went, as regular as a metronome.

The spite of it. "Fourteen," May thought, "you'd think I never was that age at all." It was hard to think that far back to the girl people called silly. Any time she'd tried to enter an opinion, her brother used to say, "You don't know," and, besides being shut up, she got some comfort from the feeling that if he could say that then he did know. If someone could know, then someone else had a chance to figure things out, too. But just now she had figured out from something as simple as Miss Gracie's face that the girl could say, "You don't know," without knowing anything better than her own bad feelings. There was nothing reassuring in it except the fact that between fourteen and thirty-five a little even narrow living might teach a person that there was more to the world than the small part of it that touched her. "I still don't know," she thought. "I go on guesses. But I don't settle for something that makes the guessing easier either." She looked up as her brother had when he was looking inward, but saw only Leslie Swanson's window and a lot of other windows just like his.

Because she had only cheap porkchops for dinner, she glazed them and made appetizers so Mr. Greene wouldn't mind. She didn't try out her ideas about Miss Gracie on him because she knew just what he would say; even though, when she told him no more piano lessons, all he did was pinch the soft part of her shoulder and say, "I hoped to hear the end of those scales."

"I didn't say no more practicing," she said.

She was thinking that Leslie Swanson never was a reason to improve her speech. He was just an excuse. There must be some reason of her own and as hard to say as her reasons for ballet and French and piano or she wouldn't be so self-conscious. Before hearing "You don't know" as a simple expression, she had thought her brother must have died knowing the reason and that what he'd said, if she could just remember specifics, would teach her. Sometimes she felt deaf, but never deaf like Beethoven, knowing music.

But Beethoven was fifty-seven when he died and she was only thirty-five and her brother had never got past twenty-six. She still had his letter telling with humor about how he'd cut off his toe trying to kill an ant with a knife, then went away to make a sound and wrap it so no one would know, and asking how long ago he'd had a tetanus shot. He was always more sensitive about what might happen, like an injection, than what he was right in the middle of, and that was what killed him. She told people he was nineteen when it happened, and she didn't know exactly why she couldn't say the truth, except that if he'd been nineteen he would have had his shot in time.

It was Miss Gracie's saying that everybody was right that made her think she'd been getting off with an easy version of why, just the way she didn't want to make a risk of melody. There was more to it, if she could just say what, and not knowing was no way to change it. "If it's dirt at the bottom of this," she thought, "it's not Kate's kind of dirt. You can keep going through it and just get deeper and deeper and deeper."

Her Book

Three times the child had come to the Home and each time, as far as she remembered, her mother had told her that someday she would understand—someday when you're a woman, her mother said. She said this in the office, quick before the sound of Mrs. Vincent coming cut her off, and Becca already understood. Her mother, a woman, was good enough for men, but someone stiff and old like Mrs. Vincent, who was a widow and wouldn't understand, was only good enough for children. It was a secret between Becca and her mother. "I *do* understand," Becca said. Through the window she'd seen the way her mother met a man and turned him around with her hands and walked away, guiding him with words and light touches and looks. This was the way she steered Becca, too, and Becca knew what came next, that pretty soon her mother would be giving up everything for that man, and nobody giving up a thing for her. It was an unfair fact of the secret that nobody gave up anything for a woman, only made a little fairer by the fact that a woman could choose the ones she wanted to give up to. Mrs. Vincent could not. Becca could not—even if being a woman would make her understanding, understanding, in keeping with the general unfairness of giving up and getting, somehow didn't make her a woman, and, until she was one, she didn't have a choice. "I *am* a woman," she told her mother. "Right," her mother said, "and I'm the Queen of Sheba," and Mrs. Vincent came, and Becca settled in for the long wait between now and someday, when she would surely also know what Sheba was.

"Do you remember Mr. and Mrs. Wrigley?" Mrs. Vincent said. "The nice people who came to see you? The nice lady with the yellow hair?" This was so long after Sheba that Becca had forgotten everything except the waiting, and it didn't occur to her yet that she was being asked to remember more than who the Wrigleys were, which was easy, because they were the only people she'd ever met who were named after chewing gum and, perhaps because of that, were different from other people. Mrs. Wrigley talked just with her hands. Only Mr. Wrigley understood what she was saying. Even when her hands were tired and rested for a while on Mr. Wrigley's arm, they said something that no one else could see but Mr. Wrigley understood. He covered them with one of his and smiled a smile that knew.

"How would you like to go and live with them?" Mrs. Vincent said. "Would you like to be their little girl?"

At first Becca didn't see in this much more than what she saw in most of Mrs. Vincent's questions—the possibility of answering yes or no, with some trouble either way. If, for instance, Mrs. Vincent asked, "Is this the way we put away our toys?" Becca knew at once that no was the right answer but meant that she'd done something wrong. She'd found that the safest way to answer Mrs. Vincent's tricky questions was not to answer them at all, to wait till Mrs. Vincent went away and then to secretly, quickly change whatever was the matter.

But this time, long and hard as she stared at the buckle on Mrs. Vincent's belt, and this was a long time for the buckle to stay put, Becca couldn't see a thing that she could do about the question. She could just be right or wrong, and for once she didn't know which was which, so she stole a look up. Mrs. Vincent was staring back at her. She was waiting, too. Mrs. Vincent didn't know the answer.

"Don't be stupid, child," she said, "the Wrigleys are much nicer than what you've known."

In a panic, Becca said, "Yes." She said it in a whisper, like a promise that she meant completely, not because she knew or cared that the Wrigleys were nicer, or thought that Mrs. Wrigley was almost as pretty as her mother and certainly much prettier than Mrs. Vincent, or wanted to find out what her hands meant. She was afraid that any second Mrs. Vincent would see the mistake, that she couldn't choose whose she was until she was a woman. She had to say something before Mrs. Vincent saw. She had to choose as if she could, and maybe sneak past waiting into knowing. Yes was as good as no.

Then, "That's right," Mrs. Vincent said and smiled, and Becca only knew that she'd been tricked again. Mrs. Vincent knew the answer all along.

There was something old about the child, in her pinched little plain face a sober and attentive patience that Melissa had seen before in children who weren't even old enough to know what was or wasn't childlike. The child's history confirmed it: Something that she wasn't even old enough to know she'd missed had to be made up to her.

In the first week of her treatments, when she'd had to stay at the hospital, Melissa had visited the wards where the chronically and catastrophically and terminally ill children were. She'd held crying infants and taken them for stroller rides, wheeling their I.V.'s along, and brought storybooks to the bedridden children and meant to do more but, after two weeks of this, returned to her own room for what she thought of as a prolonged, guilty cowering. In the faces of so many of the sick children she'd seen such a strange and knowing patience, older than anything she knew, that among them she couldn't stand her own good fortune—the years of ignorance as good as health, even the cancer caught in time merely because an accident happened to put her in the hospital, happened to focus a doctor's attention on her throat. The children didn't have the ignorance to look back on and love; they didn't know the meaning of recovery.

The girls' dormitory at the Home, where she and Cal weren't allowed till everything had been decided, looked into, and signed, reminded her of the children's ward—the cool, overhead lighting, the frameless beds and steel bureaus in neat rows against the walls, with the scattered stuffed toys and bright coverlets and paintings in pastel highlighting instead of softening the institutional order of the place. She missed only the smell and the racket—of visitors and nurses, and of children, and it took her a minute to see Becca sitting behind a bed at the far end of the room. Like a little hitchhiker, she was sitting on a suitcase, slumped, with her elbows on her knees and her hands hanging. When she heard their footsteps, she straightened up without looking around, pulled her legs together, clasped her hands on one knee, and waited.

Cal hunkered in front of her and tapped her clasped hands with one finger. "Well, Becca?" he said. "Are you going to come home with Mrs. Wrigley and me?"

"Yes," Becca said. Delicately, as if she were touching glass, she put her hand in Cal's big palm.

When they'd visited, she hadn't seemed affectionate, she'd seemed almost untouchable inside her tension, but now she held Cal's hand and walked so close that she bumped him a few times with her foot and hip; then, as he turned back after a last word from Ina Vincent, she tipped her head slightly so that her temple brushed his wrist. Melissa looked from this to Cal's face, and he smiled. Once, while he was translating a question she'd signed, the child had winked at him, distinctly winked at him, and he'd been charmed. He'd been charmed and sure since then that her usual tense seriousness was only the guise of a child who hadn't found anyone to trust yet. He didn't have to say so. Melissa could see it in the way the child's charm engaged his, when he talked with enchanted common sense about what Becca needed, how it pleased him to plan again.

That charmed assurance was in the restrained and serious way he asked Becca questions as he drove. He didn't talk about who he and Melissa were, what Becca might make of them, or what could come next. Instead he soberly asked the child about small matters, as he had when they'd visited her at the Home. She didn't seem to care any more now than then for small talk, for discussions of dolls or music or games or her dress or her day. With an air of indulgence that was clear anyway to Melissa, Becca smiled and answered when she could with a few words, which were mostly yes.

Almost from the second he reached the front door, Cal dropped his sober tone and started to talk at a glad, rapid pitch. The child was trying to follow him, her face pinched in that look of hard study. He showed her her room and then, before she'd had a chance to see what he said was hers, led her out to look at the house, telling her between the living room and den about the accident that had left Mrs. Wrigley mute but not deaf, recalling Mrs. Vincent's praise of Becca's skill at reading and supposing that she would enjoy learning to read sign language, summarizing between den and dining room his and Mrs. Wrigley's conversation about what Becca might want to call them, Mrs. and Mr., Cal and Melissa, Mom and Dad if she could, and that finally was the gist of it: It was up to her. Then he started on the kitchen. Melissa signed to him: Is she hungry?

She saw Becca note this, the flicker in the child's attention before she fixed her gaze on Cal's lips, waiting for translation. Hearing the question, she nodded a slow, significant yes, and smiled, and while he recited the contents of the refrigerator, turned secretly to regard Melissa.

"She's already on your side," Cal said over his shoulder. "She's a sympathetic mute."

Melissa tapped him and signed, then, feeling Becca's stare, added: Tell her what I said.

"Mrs. Wrigley says I haven't given you a chance to say a word." With a head of lettuce in one hand and a wedge of cheese in the other, he crouched till his face was level with Becca's, and smiled an intimate apology, a smile the child mimicked exactly. Melissa took the cheese and lettuce and turned to the counter to start sandwiches. Behind her, still low, Cal said, "I went on that way when she came home after the accident. She says."

Melissa turned sharply, but caught Becca, not Cal, looking at her. She touched her heart and smiled, but the child's intent expression didn't change.

Becca now somehow shared a house with Mr. and Mrs. Wrigley. In the house she had a room, a bed, a rocking chair, a lamp, and a desk, all of which Mr. Wrigley had given her. These things were hers, he'd said, and he'd said it so that she'd known right away that these were valuable possessions. These were valuable and hers, but in the night, after the Wrigleys left her to see exactly what she had, she'd found in the back of the desk's bottom drawer a notebook with worn edges and, tucked inside its blank pages, four torn sheets folded in half. Each of the four sheets had a message on it, two with words she didn't know, and none of which she understood, except that, because she didn't understand them, they were not for her, and nobody had given her the book that had a crushed corner and was hidden in her desk as if the desk were also someone else's, and how these things could be both hers and someone else's was something she would have to learn but suspected she already knew. They were not hers, and what she didn't know about men would fill a book. This was a book her mother had, and it didn't interest Becca half as much as the one she'd found, which mostly interested her because she'd found it and saw in its secretness some of the bigger mystery of Mr. Wrigley's connection with Mrs. Wrigley, either another part of the mystery or a clue, she didn't know which.

Mr. Wrigley was there in the morning but left after breakfast, not mad, even though when he'd tried to touch Mrs. Wrigley's hair, her yellow hair, she'd moved her head enough to put her hair out of his reach. He'd kissed her. He knew he couldn't touch Mrs. Wrigley's hair, and when he said that he would be home late, Becca saw that Mrs. Wrigley knew this, too. He was saying this aloud just for her, like the signs, because Mrs. Wrigley knew everything without having to hear it. She'd had an accident, an accident in a car, and after that she couldn't talk, but while she wasn't talking she could watch people who did and see everything before they said it. In this way, she was like Becca's mother, who'd also had an accident but could say so and could tell a person, "I know what you're thinking," though when she was asked for details, when Becca asked her, "What?" she wouldn't say, she was so mad, because she did know.

Because Mrs. Wrigley couldn't talk, a machine answered the telephone. She showed Becca the red light and small spinning reels and worked her hand like a duck quacking. Becca recognized the quacking as quickly as she saw that Mrs. Wrigley meant that the machine could talk. This was a sign that she understood, though the idea of talking as quacking was new to her and seemed to be another clue to Mrs. Wrigley that she would have to learn.

Mrs. Wrigley knew this, too. She made hand signs, then wrote down on a piece of paper: I WILL TEACH YOU. Becca had already forgotten the signs that said it, but now she knew what they meant, and knew the letters, like the letters in the book, and when she held out her hands and Mrs. Wrigley pressed them, she could feel the knowledge coming into them.

Mrs. Wrigley wrote: I WANT YOU TO BE HAPPY.

Now Becca was sure about the book. I AM HAPPY, she wrote, and underlined the AM three times as it had been on the folded message; and then, to show how well she understood, she copied out another one: I DON'T MIND.

Under this, Mrs. Wrigley wrote carefully: YOU CAN TALK. I CAN HEAR. This wasn't the answer Becca expected, especially after quacking, even though she didn't know exactly what answer she did expect—she only knew this wasn't it, and, seeing Mrs. Wrigley's hand going so slow and then her slow smile when she finally looked up, Becca was afraid she hadn't understood it after all. She wrote with a little desperation: I AM NOT CONTAGOUS. It looked right to her, but, because it was a new word, she knew it was risky and wasn't surprised when Mrs. Wrigley merely tore the full page off the pad and folded it into her pocket. Mrs. Wrigley was about to write the answer when the telephone rang and her pen jumped on the page, leaving a jagged mark. OOPS, she wrote, and nodded at the telephone, with a lift of her eyebrows and a tip of her hand asking Becca if she wanted to answer.

Right before Mrs. Wrigley punched the button on the machine, Becca heard Mr. Wrigley's voice. She waited, but when he didn't say anything else, she said, "Hello."

The strange cry that came from the phone was such a surprise that by the time Becca realized that it was her name and her mother and, with a fear a little like what she'd just felt, realized that it wasn't strange, her mother knew, Mrs. Wrigley had already taken away the phone and was listening to the rest. Her mother's voice talking to Mrs. Wrigley sounded strange again, but like quacking now, and Mrs. Wrigley put down the phone and looked at it as if it might jump up again and give her a duck bite. Looking at Mrs. Wrigley looking at the telephone, Becca was afraid in a way that was new.

They got away from the phone. They went in the car to a building downtown, and in the building went up to floor seventeen, where a woman sitting at a desk said sadly, "Oh, Melissa. You're looking for Cal? He's at the site." What Becca couldn't understand was how Mr. Wrigley could be at the site and be at the same time with her mother on the phone. It was possible that Mr. Wrigley and her mother were at the site, though she'd never known her mother to go to a site, and it was possible that Mrs. Wrigley knew this, because, though the woman at the desk gave her an address, a park and not a site was where they went and spent the afternoon with sign language between them, and something else that made either the teaching or the learning difficult.

Becca was in bed, her bed, but not asleep when Mr. Wrigley came home late. As on the phone, his voice was cut off in the middle of a word, and then, after a silence that she knew was the silence of Mrs. Wrigley talking, he said a long and disbelieving, "How?" Creeping to the door, Becca could see down the hallway most of Mr. Wrigley and most of Mrs. Wrigley's back and one of her hands working the air with fury. She was shouting. "I will," Mr. Wrigley said. "First thing in the morning."

Mrs. Wrigley said something without moving her hand.

"This late?" he said.

They moved out of sight. Listening hard, Becca heard a rustle and the jingle of the telephone being picked up and not a word until the click of it being put down again, when Mr. Wrigley said something that ended with "Becca take it?"

She looked sidelong at the shadowy room that was hers and all the shadowy, half-lit things in it that were also hers but whose value she knew only through Mr. Wrigley's voice. Only the book, deep in the drawer, was valuable without Mr. Wrigley's knowing, and that, she'd found on getting out of bed once earlier, had instead of yesterday's four messages, only one, a new one that said: HELLO, BEAUTIFUL. BEAUTIFUL was familiar and, coming after HELLO, seemed good, but now she wasn't sure.

Hearing Mr. Wrigley and Mrs. Wrigley coming down the hall, she snuck back to bed and pretended sleep as they passed by, pausing at the door, and she heard Mr. Wrigley say, "There's nothing she can do," and then, "You have to feel sorry for her." By opening her eyes only a slit, she could see for a second Mrs. Wrigley's furious face and hands, and thought again about the book—it must be good and must be hers and she could find out for sure if Mr. Wrigley would just go away again.

She woke in the dark without knowing she'd slept or that she'd heard a sound, only knowing that she was awake and what her mother called all ears. She was listening for a sound that she was afraid she'd hear again and about which listening was the only thing she could do. Even as she recognized her sleep and her room, her lamp on her desk in the dark, and knew that the deep murmur was Mr. Wrigley, the murmur was gone and Mr. Wrigley was walking past her door, down the hall. The faraway front door opened and shut.

She got out of bed and took the book out of its hiding place. Opening it in the dark to HELLO, BEAUTIFUL, she carried it down the hall to the room where Mrs. Wrigley would be. That was the master bedroom.

The half-closed door hid most of the room, but, in the mirror over the dresser, she could see what it took her a second to know was Mrs. Wrigley sitting on the bed with her yellow hair on her hand on her knee. She was completely bald. Becca had never seen a bald woman, and, when Mrs. Wrigley touched a bare spot by her ear, she knew that she wasn't supposed to. This wasn't for her to see, as the sounds that sometimes woke her weren't for her to hear, and, just as she could only listen to the sounds, she could only stare secretly at Mrs. Wrigley in the mirror and wonder whether Mr. Wrigley had done this to her or just found out what he wasn't supposed to know either. Then she saw her own face in the mirror, and jumped. Holding her book tight, she crept back down the hall, as quiet as if her creeping steps could erase the sound she'd just made, and so save Mrs. Wrigley from something.

The sight of her bald head was frightening even to Melissa, as many times as she'd seen it in these past months and as often as she'd had a chance to get used to the perplexing idea that the plucked woman reflected in the mirror was herself. Afraid she'd frightened Becca, she replaced the blonde wig and, wrapping her robe around her, went down the hall.

Becca's door was open a crack and in the pale light it let in she could see the child lying in bed with her book in one hand and her other hand held out in front of her, gesturing. Watching, she recognized a letter, then another, and others mixed in willy-nilly with invented signs—gibberish, but with inflection, phrasing, pauses between what were clearly meant to be words. She took a step back, out of sight, and knocked softly, giving Becca a second to expect her; but when she stepped forward, now into the child's stare, she feared she'd just given her one more second of dread.

After stopping at the desk to light the lamp and get a pen, dallying a little so Becca could get used to her, she went to the bed and sat down. On the blank first page of the book, she wrote: I WAS SICK. Becca looked from this to her face. Melissa added: IT WILL GROW BACK. The child's expression didn't change. Always that intent look seemed to wait for more, explanation, information, seemed to be suspending judgment. Melissa pointed to her hair, but Becca, as if she'd already forgotten that bald woman, merely frowned down and flipped through the book to the loose page with the greeting on it. She turned this around so Melissa could read.

Melissa touched Becca's cheek and with a smile tried to communicate what she meant by "beautiful." Promptly Becca took the pen and, frowning close as an apprentice forger, copied the words. As if she weren't quite sure of her work, she looked down at it for a second, considering, then added as painstakingly: I AM NOT FRAGILE. Oh, Melissa said soundlessly, and Becca quickly crossed out the E.

When the child looked up again, apprehensively, Melissa leaned slowly into her gaze and put her arms around her and, feeling in her small shoulders a tense, tentative submission, guessed that Becca was somehow attaching the significance of this embrace to those words. She wished for a minute that Becca would talk, would prattle and chatter as some children did, even some of the sick ones with her look, who seemed to think muteness meant a good listener, and out would come stories and comments and questions innocently revealing. In her arms, Becca stiffened and her hands, quick and hidden, clutched at the book between them, getting it under the edge of the sheet just as Melissa let go to see, and Cal said, "What, awake?"

He was standing at the door. He'd come back quiet as ever, and met her glance with the look he always wore, smiling and slightly bewildered, as if he'd waked wandering and were surprised that the first house he'd wandered into happened to be his. Now he had a daughter to be surprised by, too, and to look at her he tilted his head at an angle like hers on her pillow. "Did you have a bad dream, Becca?"

"Yes," she said. She said it as if she were pleased indeed to report it, and it occurred to Melissa for the first time that something had waked the child and that it hadn't been a dream. Despite her stiffening a second ago, and her book-hiding, Becca was wearing what Melissa had come to think of as her Cal expression, a look of oblique sweetness that was disturbing, and not just because it appeared so promptly when Cal did. It was familiar, but misplaced. It was, she thought, the look of a woman expecting to be asked to dance, and she wondered again what Becca'd seen of her mother's romantic life, though Ina Vincent had assured them that whenever a man entered the picture Becca entered the Home. Ina Vincent had also assured them that the mother was not told the names of the adopting parents, and that this mother wouldn't care to know, anyway—she was nesting this time. The idea of Becca's mother nesting didn't fit the picture Melissa had of her, but neither did the sound of her voice on the phone, after the wild cry, which did.

Spell "fragile," she signed to Cal, and define it.

Sitting by her on the bed, he said, "Surely you know—" but, at a look from her, cut himself off and turned to Becca to ask her nicely, "You want to know what fragile means?" He spelled it and went into an explanation, but as soon as Becca realized what word it was, her smiling attention wandered dreamily away from him until, when he was telling her that some fragile things were champagne flutes, baby chicks, thin women like Melissa, and the wrists of tiny little girls, was in fact holding the child's own, she was plainly feigning sleep.

"The woman" was her mother and she knew everything. That much Becca knew already, but at breakfast she learned from Mr. Wrigley's answers and Mrs. Wrigley's face that they were just finding this out, and it caused some confusion. It made Mrs. Wrigley frown and say so many quick things with her hands that by the time Mr. Wrigley agreed, as he did at certain times, Becca could tell from his face that he didn't remember anymore what out of so many signs he was agreeing to. Becca was collecting everything that was confusing about Mrs. Wrigley, including her hair and BEAUTIFUL and bits of Mr. Wrigley's explanation of FRAGILE and Mr. Wrigley himself, and she added this. This collection itself seemed confused, but she felt that somehow it would make sense when she understood each thing in it, just as Mrs. Wrigley's hands would make sense when she understood each sign. Then Mrs. Wrigley's hand that was saying something above Becca's ear stopped and dropped onto her shoulder, and the fear came back.

It was a fear like what she'd felt when Mrs. Vincent asked her if she wanted to be Mrs. Wrigley's little girl. Her disappointment at finding out that was a cheat had been blurred down to nothing by another possibility that had occurred to her since then with such enormity and strangeness that she couldn't think of anything to do with it but sit and wait. It was the safe sense that she could sit and wait that held together everything confusing about Mrs. Wrigley, but now it suddenly was gone and there was just confusion and to sit and wait didn't seem possible, but still she couldn't think of anything else to do. Mrs. Wrigley was going to find out that nobody could have her except someone who had an accident or a duty to the state and decency or got paid like the babysitters Jeanne and Mrs. Marker. She already knew something. It was in her hand.

It didn't help that Mr. Wrigley went away. Becca was already used to the idea that he came back. If she could think he wouldn't, she could think again that Mrs. Wrigley, because her hair came off, was in some way that she hadn't quite figured out yet like Mrs. Vincent and only good enough for children—but Mr. Wrigley's saying as he went that he was going to do something and that he would take care of it was as good as his saying he would be home late, and she could only wonder if what he was going to do was find out the mistake and come back and tell Mrs. Wrigley. He was going to find out from her mother.

When the telephone rang, Mrs. Wrigley stood with her hands in the pockets of her skirt and looked at it until the light went on. Her mother and Mr. Wrigley were on the phone, and Mrs. Wrigley had her hands in her pockets because she didn't want to pick it up and hear. The second time it rang, she only looked at it from the sofa, where she was showing Becca how to say in hand signals: I AM HUNGRY. She knew something, and in this way she was like Becca's mother when she didn't want to answer the phone either. Also like her mother, after three rings that she knew about but didn't want to answer, Mrs. Wrigley took Becca shopping.

This was the first time Becca had seen Mrs. Wrigley in a skirt, and, walking behind her through the racks of dresses, she could see that Mrs. Wrigley was as thin as Mr. Wrigley said. Then Mrs. Wrigley saw what she was thinking and wouldn't let her walk behind. To be thin was a dream her mother had. Becca was thin, sometimes as a twig, sometimes as a toothpick, sometimes as a skinny little goose, and she was lucky, but Mrs. Wrigley wasn't lucky, even though she had the accident, which was a blessing in disguise. Mr. Wrigley said. It was his fault. She wanted Mrs. Wrigley to write a note about her accident that told how it could be a blessing in disguise when her mother's wasn't, even though they both involved a car, but she was afraid that just by asking she would give something away. Maybe Mr. Wrigley would take her mother in a car and get her in an accident and then she would go to the hospital, where something else would happen that would make her bald. That would be a blessing in disguise. She spelled out with her hands: I AM HUNGRY.

Mrs. Wrigley had been frowning for a long time at a dress that Becca knew would fit her, and now she put the dress away and, with a new look and the touch of her fingertips on Becca's shoulder, told her they were done shopping. Becca led the way back to the car and climbed onto her seat and fastened her seat belt. It wasn't until she saw speeding past her window a dog and then a yellow house she thought she knew that she started to think in a hurry fast as everything was going by that she might have got the signs wrong, and the look wrong, and the touch. Then she saw the house and Mr. Wrigley already opening the door and felt all down her back the lurch the car made when it stopped.

Even without seeing them, she knew what the signs Mr. Wrigley made over her head meant. When Mrs. Wrigley put her hands away in her pockets, Becca knew he'd made the signs. He took her to her room, then, and, showing her a book about three bears, said that she might like to read it and that he would like it very much if she would read it for a while. When he left she put the book back on the shelf where it belonged and snuck down the hall to the corner.

He was already saying something in his murmur. He was telling Mrs. Wrigley about the mistake, but she didn't believe him. Suddenly he said right over Mrs. Wrigley's moving hands, "I *tried.*" Nothing else was clear until the words "*talk* to her" burst out loud at the end of a murmur, and Mrs. Wrigley's mouth said, "We?" without a sound.

"I will," he said, "I know you don't . . ." and got so close to Mrs. Wrigley that Becca couldn't even hear the murmur anymore. It was like being pressed between them, squeezed in a dense space where nothing was clear, and, when the pressure dropped away, she didn't even know if she'd heard Mr. Wrigley say it: She is the child's mother. Watching from a distance as Mrs. Wrigley disagreed and Mr. Wrigley murmured an answer with "nature" in it and Mrs. Wrigley's hand hardened and cut the air, she only knew as clearly as if she'd heard it said in words that Mr. Wrigley hadn't talked to her mother, yet. He hadn't talked to her, but he was going to, and it would be soon. She could see it coming in the gradual, grudging slowing down of Mrs. Wrigley's hand, which finally settled into complete stillness on Mr. Wrigley's arm.

She didn't know who saw it first, but with a start they were both looking at the window, and she knew it was her mother. Mr. Wrigley moved, but Mrs. Wrigley caught his arm and said something in hurried signs. "Honey," he said, as her mother said that word when she wanted something that was just not fair. He wrapped his hand around the signing one till it was quiet and the other one let go his arm. Before he opened the door, he looked back. His face was like her own face in the mirror looking at Mrs. Wrigley bald.

From Ina Vincent's words, Melissa had made up a picture of Becca's mother that was as far from anything the prim widow would say about a woman as it was from Melissa. That was the picture's allure, a dark and ravening seductiveness that would consume itself again and again while Melissa watched, and every time she'd remade the image she'd given something more of herself to it, some of her color, some of her heat, her voice.

But here was an almost homely girl, softly plump, honey blonde, squinting a little at the numbers on the houses. It was the softness Melissa saw first, the clumsy grace of the girl's limbs, her figure, her full, fair face that, along with the intensity of her near-sighted look, made her seem to be a combination of mother and child, everything the picture wasn't.

Cal met her on the walk and she looked past him at the house. She'd stopped squinting and turned her concern into a pretty look, catlike and alert. When she took a step, Cal politely cupped her elbow, and she stopped, she turned her head at a slight tilt to look up at him and say something that Melissa couldn't read. She seemed to be asking him a question. As the girl turned back toward the house, Melissa could see the gentle tug of Cal's hand on her arm and then the way the girl as if according to some natural law gave in, took a small, turning step that wasn't a step at all but brought her elbow roundly into his big hand. He was leading her away from the house, talking, talking, talking, his head canted toward her, serious and fatherly as a priest giving counsel, and the girl's head inclined so slightly that the only sign of it was the sway and brush of her fair hair against his shoulder for a second.

Melissa started. Becca'd brushed her leg. She'd come up without a sound and was standing next to her, watching through the window. Melissa's instinct reached before she did to pull the child away, and she was only starting to bend and extend her hand, when she saw Becca's face and stopped. The child was fascinated. She was watching the scene outside with a look as keen and exacting as the one she had for sign language and letters, her attention working so hard on one thing that it didn't even take in Melissa's movement.

Melissa was as careful as she'd ever been. The tension she'd felt every time she'd touched the child was visible now. It was in the little girl's thrilled stillness—and then, in the way that stillness snapped and she suddenly turned, clumsy in her quickness, bumping Melissa's leg and shifting, quick, impatient, patting the ballooning skirt aside as Melissa stooped to her. It was in her eyes, a look so bright it seemed almost demonic, as she whispered, "I understand." Her delighted, knowing little face was slyly like that discarded picture of her mother, and, with a cry, bated and soundless, Melissa gave up to it altogether.

Arriving in the Dark

The man's child was also his sister, though, never having had a sister and certainly not a child and with no one around to teach him, he understood only in the most primitive way that she was his, because she had been left to him and nobody else. How she'd come to be was something that he understood in a primitive way, too. From childhood into a sorry sort of manhood he had been raped by his father, who owned the land for miles around. The boy had only rarely seen other people on the land, and those few he saw showed great deference to his father, as seemed natural to the boy, who was used to the same deference in himself and in his mother. From the man the boy learned that these people, other people, were not to be spoken to or trusted, and to the end of his life, long after he'd learned that his father was the one who shouldn't have been trusted, the distrust of speech and other people lasted; but at the time, when the lessons took, the boy had no one to tell him that what the man taught him was not within a father's natural rights.

The man forced himself upon his son, who so far only comprehended pain as punishment and so wept over being hurt as badly as he was but also over not knowing what wrong he'd done to earn it. Soon enough, however, the man taught his son that he could forget the pain by performing the same operation on him, and this was how the boy learned that pain might also be a means of earning pleasure. Without thinking much about it, the boy also assumed that the man had the same arrangement with his mother, whom he often heard weeping at night. So he grew up feeding his sex into his father and believing this was how it worked.

He was underneath his father one night when the man convulsed and fell down flat upon him as he usually did, but this time without slackening or moving to withdraw or in fact moving anymore at all. When the boy realized that his father was not going to move, he tried to get loose, only to find himself pinned, and this was how he stayed until morning, when his mother discovered them and helped to pry him and the man apart. Those that live by the sword, she said.

For a time then a few more strangers appeared, to make funeral arrangements and to settle affairs that the boy had never known existed, affairs that made him a rich man, though he didn't understand yet what that meant, except that he had to go into town, where he was the stranger, and sign his unaccustomed name to papers in a place where people treated him with the same deference that they had always shown his father.

Grievously confused, he knew at least that everything had changed because he was left lying alone every night with his head full of all the strangeness that he'd recently encountered and no one to explain to him what any of it meant. In his confusion and his pain, like none he'd ever had, he missed his father, and so at night he took to wandering and, passing his mother's dark door, he heard her crying and he thought it was the same for her. He went into the room and sat down on the bed and patted his mother's arm; he didn't know many caresses. Then his mother opened her arms to him, so he lay down with her and soon was trying to do what he knew ended pain, but she shifted and took him in where she was wet and looser than he was used to and with her back to him and her arms clasped around her knees she murmured every time he pushed into her, Yes, this is where you belong.

It was too late for him to learn what she meant by that. When he finished she was still weeping but because she was differently equipped than him and his father he didn't know how else to bring her relief, so he learned instead that for women there was only pain. This was difficult for him to accept because he didn't understand hurting for pleasure with no pain to himself, and, though he kept going in to his mother out of need and sorrow, he was moving toward a horror of women's crippled pleasure, as he saw it, that the birth of the child made complete, because he was there to see it.

The emergence of the baby from between his mother's legs, where she had taken him in, was the final evidence, after the horrible swelling of the thing inside her, that the pain they were made for was too much for women to bear. Through the birth his mother screamed like no animal he'd ever heard and he tried to help by doing what she told him, but most of the time she couldn't tell him anything, and finally he couldn't listen to her screaming anymore and ran away.

When he came back, it was to silence. He couldn't wake his mother or move her to tell him what to do with the baby lying in a pool of slime between her legs. It was alive, this much he knew. Out of loneliness and a disgust of filth more than anything else, he washed the baby, which quickly learned to cry.

He had been taught acceptance early on, and, because he was still a long way from finding out that he had learned too much of it, he was inclined to see the baby as a fact of nature like any other, a reward or a punishment or task, but not a matter of indifference as long as it was crying. The fact that he found himself alone with only this somewhat human thing inspired in him the sense that it had to be kept secret or the other people that he distrusted anyway would want to take it from him when they found that it was all that had come of the pain he'd caused his mother. This was the form his distrust had taken, a belief that strangers naturally wanted to take away what he had, and just the notion that he was in danger of losing the baby was enough to make it seem worth keeping for a while.

He had to ride for nearly a full day to find a town far enough away for him to feel safe asking strangers about babies. The response of women further convinced him of the value of the child. As best he could, which was not well but adequately, he did the things the women said or at least did what he imagined they meant. He fed the baby and he changed and washed it, and this was just the sort of work he needed to confirm him in his suspicion that the child was his and nobody else's concern.

What he wasn't prepared for was the affection. Awkward as he was, afraid of touches except the rough kind he'd received at his father's hands and even more afraid now of the soft sort that his mother had administered, he did not hold or caress the baby. When he washed or changed it, he did so as efficiently as he could, and then he laid her on the bed and looked at her. He didn't speak to her either—at this time simply because it seemed a stupid effort to waste speech, so suspect anyway, on a speechless thing. However, it was not long before the baby began touching him. It reached out and it grabbed at him and chugged its legs as if it wanted to spring backward on the bed. Its head moved like a squirrel's, looking at everything, and if he left the room for one thing or another it might stop crying upon his return, or sometimes even coo. Now when he tried to dress the baby, it would interfere with wonder, cry at having its face covered even for an instant as the gown went on, and grip his hands as they pulled its own into the sleeves. And so, little by little, because its behavior began to seem as much a command of nature as anything else, the baby taught him how to hold it. How to hold her—he had given himself time in concluding that the baby was going to be like his mother and never grow equipment like his own, and this seemed significant to him, as if nature had given him a girl so he could make up for killing his mother. The child began to seem like a gift, with grave responsibilities attached.

It was at about this time that he was also beginning to understand that he would have to go out in the world; it was either that or people would come here, which was unacceptable. His father's bank and business people had taken care of his affairs for a long time now, and from them he had learned a bit as they'd advised him on immediate problems, the mysterious business behind daily life, but now they were insisting that he assume his father's role, which he still could not quite understand, except that he could pay someone to do most of the understanding. His slight understanding so far was such that the people he needed for it seemed to control the money that he needed for it, too, so their insistence was too much for him and he knew he had to do what they said.

All his feelings and experience struggled against this, and all the power of his longing not to go anywhere else fixed upon the child. All the sadness and the anger of his sense that he was going to have to leave her went into his care of her, stronger every day as he saw the time coming.

This was when he decided to guard the girl from any speech. The world had tried to overwhelm him once by delivering the child to him, and now it was in the form of the child herself that the same world would not be able to touch him. He hadn't even learned yet what sort of corruption his father had practiced, but already he knew that the girl couldn't be on the receiving end of any pain like that, and especially she could not die screaming while what a man would want to put into her came bursting back out, a baby. He had a literal imagination and could only see this horror happening to the child as she was now, too tiny and fragile to be considered, so he knew this could not be, and he determined to keep her apart from anyone or anything that could hurt her.

With this decision, the notion of going away became bearable, and he began to look for a woman to watch over the child. He was still a long way from fearing women as well for the girl's sake, as he would do when he saw how they conjured up the very need from which he was determined to protect her, and he was further still from hating them, as would happen, too, when he discovered that there was no help for it.

In his father's car the man drove almost the full day again, to where he'd had his questions answered once, to find the old woman who couldn't speak and couldn't hear all that well either. She was just what he had been looking for. Sexless as she seemed to him, and silent, she wouldn't interfere with him and couldn't corrupt the child and didn't seem to care about leaving the world behind, which in his eyes made her trustworthy. It was on the land that all the horrors had happened to him, but these were his horrors and his land, all he really knew, and so the populated rest of the world presented a threat to just what stood for understanding in him; what he knew he knew in such complete isolation that it meant life itself to him and so everything else meant nothing, the strangeness and the loneliness of death, and one instinct that had never been perverted or weakened in him was the instinct to stay alive.

The woman had no husband and her two children were grown up and gone away, as she signed to him in answer to his questions. About her husband's death she elaborated by chopping her neck with the sharp side of her flattened hand, then dropping her head to the side. This she did with no change in her expression, a coolness, though there was a hint of melancholy in the way she constantly watched as her hands moved. For the children, she merely raised her hands in front of her, a foot or so above her head, then either made them into wings flying away or dismissed them with a wave on either side, he couldn't tell which and either way didn't know whether this meant that the two big children were gone away or dead, but both were acceptable, so it didn't matter. No trespassers, he told her, assuming his father's role, and anybody but himself was a trespasser. This seemed acceptable to her, too, another sign of her trustworthiness.

He indicated to the woman that she should come with him, and she followed along but stopped a second, staring at the car. From her hesitation, he assumed that she knew his father; she recognized the car or knew he was too rich for it or even suspected the worst of what he did—so when she creakily climbed into the car anyway, he trusted that he would never have to bring her back again.

When the young man had come for her, the woman had been unprepared and yet ready as ever to leave behind a less than satisfactory life if someone were going to give her a chance. It had been so long since she had given up the dream of being rescued by a handsome young man, so long the forgotten dream had even left off fastening on her sons, who between them had enough beauty for one but had lately done more for the hardship she hoped to escape than for her hope of ever getting away—it had been so long, at any rate, that she was as annoyed as she was pleased to see this stranger, because he'd turned up after all, but twenty-five years too late.

And when he showed her to his car, she could not believe that he wanted her to ride in it, much less that once she did she would never return, a likelihood entirely in keeping with her feelings about automobiles, especially those that, like this one, looked as if only magic might hold them together. Here the young man was, however, after all those years of forgetting that there were such things as sudden changes; so when he opened the door on the passenger side, which faced the little house where she had her one room, the stacks of laundry and mending waiting in it as they would forever, though in time they would see some altering that no one had ever asked her to do, she went ahead. She let herself be handed up and she sat herself down on the cracked leather seat and, with her hands folded on her lap, as they always folded to hold each other steady through their rare rest, rode away.

Hours later, after the sun had long set on country that she'd never seen before, she started to suspect that she should have packed some things. Clearly she had agreed to an arrangement that she hadn't altogether understood, but, because her agreement had been asked for, she was not particularly worried, except about how she would tell her boys, when they might want to reach her, where she was, because she didn't know and didn't know how to ask and there turned out to be no one to ask anyway.

They went through woods, across a field, and then uphill through woods again, so far that she hadn't noticed an electric light or even a wire overhead for so long that she didn't know when she'd started noticing, and then they came to a house. Around the house there was a clearing, and no wires here either, or any light besides the car's. The headlights showed her a two-story building made of weather-beaten wood with narrow windows and a dark porch all around the bottom like a big grin of pain. After the man turned off the car, everything was black, but he came around and opened the door for her and led her to the house, up the steps and to the door, as sure-footedly as if it were bright daylight out. Count on a man to know his way around the dark.

Right inside he lit a lamp. Even in the poor light she could see that the hall where she found herself was grim out of stupidity, as only a man could possess, though this one was at least neat. She saw not a speck of dirt on the wooden floor, the corners dustless angles, too, but no rug either, and the hall had been trod into one long sag.

The walls, covered with lined paper, were so grimy to see that only out of heroic politeness was she able to keep from putting her hands into her clean pockets.

The man left the lamp he'd lighted on the newel post, where a ball or something like had been knocked off, perhaps for just this purpose. Then he conducted her through a small room of shadows into a larger darker one, where he lit lamps fixed to the walls on either side of the door.

A little girl was lying on a sofa on the other side of the room. She lay face down with her hands curled up by her ears, one wrist tied, the loose line strewn all over the floor and leading finally to the window frame and tied there where the wood bowed out. The child was a sight. Her hair was like a wad of carded wool, tied with a string behind her head, and she was wearing a dress many times too big for her, also gathered up with a string around the waist but not well enough to have kept the hem from being frayed to the point of fringe, the dirty little bare feet sticking out below. Also, there was the stench of an accident.

The man laid his arm across the door to stop her. Then without making a noise, he slowly approached the sofa. Even though he was too quiet for the woman to hear, the little girl woke up. She sprang at the man and clung to him, and the woman could see her weeping but could barely hear a sound from her, only one like a soft shuddering aloud. Still clinging with one arm and with her face buried in the man's neck, the child held out her tied wrist like an old-time movie queen offering her hand to be kissed. As he went about the task of untying the string, the man's face, carved out of the dark by the lamplight, was grim. It looked like the girl's embrace brought him to the edge of a dangerous anger or pain.

The three of them went outside then, the man leading with a lantern to a rank outhouse next to a line of three old holes unhoused and capped. The woman watched while he wiped the child with the odd diaper she had been wearing, much too old for that, made of what she couldn't tell, then tossed the whole thing into the stool.

Leading with the light again and with the little girl in hand and hugging up against his leg, which gave his weighted walking the look of a limp, the man took them back inside and up the stairs into a long windowless hall. He paused at the first door and pointed to himself, then went on to the next and pointed to the woman but didn't give her a minute to look in before he walked on to the last room and took the little girl in there.

The way the child clung to her father when he put her into bed, no washing up or nightclothes either, just the same dirty strung-up dress, was like a woman knowing her man was going away, if any woman was ever sure enough of a man to cling to him like that, and he let her. He sat waiting until the girl wore out. Only her eyes were still awake and in the dim light, as the man bent to retrieve the lantern, the woman saw the eyes on her, wild and fearful and longing to know what she was.

The room where the man left the woman, with a sign to the lamp and matchbox lying nearby, was made up, a neat bed and a pitcher of water sitting in a big chipped bowl beside, as if he knew she would be coming back with him, even though she'd never seen him till today. The closet, big enough to walk in, with a curtain for a door, was even full of women's clothes. They were dresses she might have worn when she was younger, plain and the right size for a woman tall as she had been, but, now that she was starting to stoop and fill out in the slow way of people tending downward into a last lumpishness before they joined the earth, they probably would be too long and too high in the waist, but she could take them up and let them out. This was something she could do. She laid herself down sure of the chore, after the uncertainty of the little girl, who was a piece of work she wasn't sure she understood.

Lying in the dark, she recalled the diaper being dropped into the hole. This wasteful practice had dismayed her more than the babyish needs of the girl, who she guessed must be slow in the way of people who lived in the woods, breeding like animals and producing beasts.

Her own boys were also beasts, though there was nothing beast-like in the breeding of them except her husband's nighttime behavior, which was the way it went, she knew, and, even if it wasn't to her liking nearly as much as the man's daytime way of going off to work that he seemed to know all along would kill him in the end, she had to respect it anyway, because she couldn't help it any more than the man could help the perpetrating of it, so she was disappointed slightly not to see some of it in the sweet one, Doug, and she couldn't help respecting the more than enough of it that she saw in the other one, John.

The two of them were beasts, but not at all alike. Between the two they had enough to make up one animal of a man. Doug had got the dumb-beast portion, the plodding-oxen part of manhood, while his brother had got all the wildness. This was why they stuck together, different as they were. She saw in Doug the same helplessness that she felt in mothering John, even when she knew being a mother ought to mean disgust at what he did to other sons and daughters, but with that one she was somehow a woman first. And then she saw in John the animal smartness of knowing that he needed the animal helplessness of them both, her and Doug, because he would use everyone else up.

Since they had left home only a year before, the boys had already lived together in three towns, moving each time John got into trouble, Doug always the one to get him out and get him started once more. Each time it happened, they would come home first and John would tell her what had happened, and she would get angry at whatever girl was in the story, in part because she knew without the girl there wouldn't be the story, but mostly because she had to blame a girl who couldn't see trouble coming, which was as good as inviting trouble into the already troubled enough world of women without the one consolation, the taming of day. There had to be a girl somewhere to take over the womaning of her wild son.

Now when they came home she would not be there. For the first time it occurred to her that here she might be doing something for the troubled world and for once she saw how without John to worry about she might miss Doug most of all.

When the woman woke, the girl was at her door, with the same alert bewildered look in her eyes, and, though she wouldn't let the woman close enough to touch her, she stayed only a pace or two away, scuttling back a step whenever the woman paused or made a sharp move. Like this the two of them discovered that the man was gone, the car was gone, the kitchen—one with an old cookstove the likes of which the old woman had never worked and a huge washtub—was stocked with food, everything dry or smoked or canned. Fires were banked in two of the downstairs rooms, and outside there was a woodpile, enough to last for a long time. For a minute the woman considered that the man might be a witch, because how else could he have been so sure of her that he could leave fires like that, but then she dismissed the notion, considering that, even if she hadn't come or wouldn't stay, the fires would've been made anyway, because this was a hard man of silence and probably sorrow who was as ready every day to die or go away as he was to stay.

By the time the man came back, in perhaps a week, she had cleaned and worked her way into a place so secure that she could draw a list of pictures of the things she wanted for the house and for the girl and herself and present it to him like a bill. This was when he showed her to the other house, a walk away. It was run-down and dark, a kitchen and two rooms that looked like pioneer material, and, though she didn't like it much because it seemed like an insult to progress, she felt she'd earned it with her trustworthy week of work and so it must have some value, even if only in the deserving. She made a point of putting some of her adopted things from the big house into the little one and keeping it clean, neat, and ready.

At first the child needed attention all the time. She was used to it from the man but not used to anyone else, so she would occupy herself always in the woman's way, demanding that the woman look or stumble on her everywhere she went, but for a long time not allowing her near enough to do anything with her. It was almost a month before, instead of planting herself in the woman's path, always a few feet ahead, the girl began to sneak up behind her, touch her, and then run away to her usual distance, ahead again once the woman had turned, surprised and then, after a while, in habit, as if they were a little wind and a weathercock working in reverse, until the girl stopped running and in time the woman stopped turning and the two of them settled into a way of being easily next to each other. After that the girl tolerated lessons in washing up and changing clothes and helping out with simple chores. The woman had once adopted a stray dog that wouldn't leave but out of some stray instinct or habit of distrust wouldn't become a pet either, and this wasn't all that different. They had something to do with each other, like a couple of strangers both abandoned on an island, and they made the natural and necessary accommodations without getting close enough to pry into why the other was in such a state.

Eventually it became clear that the man wanted his daughter to be as much of a lady as such a nameless wild thing could be. He brought the best of what the woman drew for him, as if to show her how much he welcomed her help in things he couldn't think of first, and, as the girl's progress in cleaning and dressing and behaving herself started to show, he would smile and pet her in approval of each step, so the girl would do to the extreme whatever she had done before her father's visit, because she clearly thought it would bring him back to hold her. For so skittish a creature, so begrudging of touching with the woman, she was strangely sweet and clinging with her father. Otherwise the woman would have guessed the man had hit her just as someone must have hit the untouchable stray. But now it looked to her like just the opposite, the child so touched and tended by the man with no one else around that she had come to think he was all that her affection was for.

Hearing had given the woman speech to think in, but the girl had nothing like it. Though she heard, there were only weather, animal noises, and her own odd sounds to learn as a language, so she thought mostly in the terms of touch and sight, with sound as an accompaniment, because that was how it made sense. A bird for her was color, shape, and flight with a particular noise telling her where and when to look. Once a cat came onto the land. She knew to stay away from the dogs that haunted the place, her father had made sure of that, but the cat was more approachable in size and in the silky way it walked, and she came to believe she and the creature were related because it mewed out the same sound she sometimes made in her own throat. However, that was a mistake. After watching for a while, she made the mewing sound herself and the cat only went away and soon it went away from her dreams, too, where it had for a time made mysterious appearances as the keeper of secrets. It was a messenger from the world outside her own, which she was only gradually coming to suspect with the suspicion that it was the place of all things that were not constant in her life, the place of certain birds in winter and others in summer, where the weather went to change and where her father disappeared to, with the automobile and the cat. From this place came new clothes and food. When it had been only her father going away and giving her the idea in the first place, she had wanted to go, too, because he himself became the place then and because he was most of what she knew, she was as good as lost if he left her. But then she'd learned he would come back. She found she could make sure of this by learning from the woman, though there remained always the shadow of a fear and a suspicion from her father's first time away because it had been such a slow and terrible surprise that there was no telling what else could happen like that without her even knowing till it was too late. But once she got used to bringing him back she began to understand more of her world without him and then she began to like it because it was becoming as familiar as he was, and so she didn't need to go away with him to where everything except him was strange, as it started to seem now. She had walked as far as she could, and that was far enough that any more and she would be lost and exhausted in the dark of lost and wandering sounds. A sound in the night told her there was an order that she didn't understand at all.

Her happiest times were when her father held her. She didn't know she'd taught him this, but her baby way of bringing on warmth with her own stayed with her for a while, until she learned that nothing else responded, that except for him the world was full of surfaces to attract her only to ignore her touch or repel it with chills and pricks and rash. Because of the indifference of so many things, she began to touch the soft and pliant ones in secret, the dandelion and the caterpillar and the feathers of a dead bird, as if they too would withdraw this pleasure if the others saw them giving it to her.

Moving things she did not touch; they had repaid her too often with leaping up, shrieking, and flight, anything to startle her. The woman fell into this category, moving things. She proved herself benign but not before showing that if touched she, too, would leap, so the girl learned after a long time of testing to hold still for the woman's touch, which was a lesson in itself. As the woman touched her, the girl learned to touch herself, her face with a wet rag, her hair with a comb, her body with buttoning clothes.

As the lessons proceeded inside, where there were rules for sleeping and dressing, eating and spending her time, the world outside changed, too. Once it had been a place full of rules as well, telling her what to run to and run from and where to crawl or climb or lie and when to go inside again, but, now that she knew what a real direction was and she would go outdoors all neat and clean and fed on schedule, she felt that she was in command of the small place that she occupied, minute to minute, and now all the rest was wild. If the world without was giving orders like the woman's, they were far too much for her to understand anything but the tiniest part her small order represented.

The world was rich in signals telling the man what he knew was wrong and what he wanted worse. The customary pairing of men and women hadn't been lost on him, and apparently it hadn't been lost on women either, though money somehow figured in their comprehension of the custom as it applied to him. He knew better, knew what happened to women, but they couldn't seem to stay out of his way, and soon enough he began to despise them for bringing on his bad instinct in spite of himself.

It was his one wish to spare the girl, the only good thing he was sure of anymore, so when women waylaid him he became incensed. He was inclined to beat them for inspiring the lust that endangered his daughter; but a beating wouldn't keep other women away, or the lust either, which he would have to get rid of in a woman anyway before he could go back home and see the girl.

Men, seeing what a stranger he was to the world, had helped him to find whores, and finally he found his own, a poor townswoman who would take him in her mouth for money and suck the lust out of him. But it would always come back anyway, and soon his unhappiness and anger were so overwhelming that he could not bear the touch of the woman, even her lips or tongue, and, because he still had to unburden himself, he made the woman mask herself off as much as she could with bandages and curl up face down in a ball, exposing only the hole, into which he forced the wooden handle broken off a shovel. In his anger he only found pleasure now in giving pain, although the operation was performed each time with the grim and deliberate righteousness of punishment being meted out. The woman held herself open with her own fingers so he didn't have to touch anything but himself, and, when the punishment was over and he was spent, she would also wash the wood. As long as the woman would take his money, this was an arrangement he could live with, because it reduced the notion of a woman to a hole, nothing like the girl.

But then one day when he went home and held his daughter in his lap, she wrapped her arms around him and he felt her breasts against him for the first time and with the anger rising up all he could think of was the handle of the shovel. He leapt up in a fury to think of the hurt that would come to her if she pressed her breasts against a man. She looked up startled from the floor, where she had fallen. Crouching there with her mouth open, she was just as the woman had been when he had allowed her to touch him with her lips, and this infuriated him further.

Although the old woman knew not to come in while he was visiting his daughter, he went to the door and closed it. When he turned the girl was in the middle of the room, watching him with worried eyes. She was dressed in the jumper that she always wore, and that he could see now was too small, though the old woman, who paid little attention to such things, had allowed her to keep wearing it, buttoned tight over her breasts, so he was surprised to feel them there flattened against him. Now the girl approached him slowly. She reached out and touched his arm as if he might disappear. He took hold of her shoulders to show her that she should stand still, and then he unbuttoned the front of her dress, exposing her small breasts, from which he made a point of averting his eyes with an expression of profound revulsion. She glanced down, too, then looked at his face in alarm. Without looking, he poked one of her breasts and flinched just as she did, making a clear display of the repugnance of this. She continued to appear perplexed, so he gripped her shoulders again and bent her back and spit on the offending growth. Released, she merely gazed down at herself in concern, as if expecting something to spring up where the spit had fallen. Finally he touched her nipples with his fingertips and when they immediately hardened, much to his disgust, he pincered them between his nails. At that she cried out at last and covered her breasts with her hands. He nodded his approval, stroked her hair and motioned her to button up and cover herself more completely.

As she sat next to him later and when he kissed her good-by, she was careful not to rub against him, so he departed confident that the lesson had succeeded, and then he went to the poor woman in town.

After that he didn't go home half as often.

The boys had found their old mute mother in a simple fashion after all. On their way to yet another town they had come home to her as usual, and, finding everything there undisturbed but dusty, they had waited and were still there when the man stopped by to gather some of her possessions, as indicated in one of her picture lists. Although he had the list and her key as proof of the old woman's well-being, the man could not convince the boys that their mother was fine, wanting no visitors, even kin. Finally he agreed to take them to her if they would keep to the conditions he laid out, to go with him at night and see their mother in good health and go away at once, never to return. It was his property and anything else would be trespassing, which he could punish on his property as he saw fit. If their mother wanted to see them again, he said she could come to them, but it wasn't likely because she had work to do. This interested them, this mysterious devotion on their mother's part, but not nearly as much as the vast dark property where the man took them to find her. "Is this it?" one of them said when they went from the real road to a dirt one, through a gate, and he said, "Yes." Fifteen minutes or more later, when they were still driving with no light around anywhere, the boy said again, with all the disbelief of someone who had never owned so much as a patch of dirt, "Is this it?" But the man didn't say any more.

He stopped at a dark cabin and let them in and left them there to wait another quarter of an hour until their mother, carrying a lantern, came to them alone. In the language they had developed between them, they learned that she was a caretaker in another house on the same property. From the way she stood apart they knew they were not welcome, as the man had said, and from the way she took a step and leaned against them to be kissed good-by they knew she thought that she might never see them again, but they couldn't tell how well she felt about this, because they couldn't quite believe it. Instead they thought there must be something underhanded in the arrangement. She leaned an extra minute against Doug, looking at him with a special sadness, and this in particular struck John as a bad sign.

Then she left them in the dark and the man came back to take them away again. He was bigger than either of them but that wasn't what made them mind him. There was something dark in his demeanor that told them that this truly was his property in such a way that while they were on it they would have no power whatsoever against him if he should decide they didn't belong here even for an instant. Riding off, they were aware as they had never been of being in their mother's care.

When they did come back, enough time had passed for some forgetting. Needing to disappear, they remembered only enough of their mother's care and the man's power to recall the long dark way there and back as leading to safety.

John had gotten carried away once more, starting with a woman again, but this time even the carrying away had gotten out of hand and there was a man dead at the end of it. John did feel bad about this, though he also felt that it was not his fault because he had been pushed to the point of not knowing what he was doing and after that he couldn't answer for his actions, and he had to blame the man for pushing him, when, if a woman could be had, it had to be and had nothing to do with any other man, no matter what he thought his stake was; but John knew as well that nobody else would see it this way, because someone had to be blamed whenever bad happened and with the blameworthy man dead he was the only one left.

Doug felt worse. He took the blame upon himself because he

knew better but couldn't help going along with his brother, and this weakness was for him the worst thing of all. What his brother couldn't help had at least the strength of nature behind it; even a good and mostly well-behaved dog knew enough to do what John did and Doug never had the heart for. He knew that if he were attacked John would fight for him, and this was like having an important part of his nature living in somebody else. Sometimes he considered it ugly, the ugly part to go with his ugly face, but sometimes it just seemed like strength and he thought he was ugly merely because he was missing it. When they needed to run and John brought up their mother's place, this struck Doug as the strength again, because he himself would never have suggested it after their one trip out, which he remembered almost as a death. John, however, even remembered the directions, after all that time and in the dark.

As they pulled up to the cabin, John said, with some memory of the man coming back, "We have to hide the car." But the area was too dark and strange for them to see where a safe hiding place might be, so they parked the car among some trees behind the little house and, shining a flashlight ahead, went inside, where, with two beds made up and water in the pot and wood stacked ready in the fireplace, everything seemed to be saying: Make yourself at home; as if their mother never really meant for them to stay away so long. John felt confirmed in this when she came in the next morning and wasn't even surprised to find them, though Doug saw it differently. "She must have figured a long time ago that she couldn't get shut of us," he said.

"Just like I was saying," John said, and Doug let it go at that.

Their mother brought them food. There was something changed about her. Although she'd always known her mind, even if she couldn't speak it, she'd never been quite so clear as she was now or never seemed so sure they would do what she told them with her hands, which seemed to cover everything around as far as they could see or guess with flat DO NOTS. "Looks like being a caretaker went right to her head," John said. "She thinks she owns the place."

Again Doug saw something else in it, but this time he didn't say what he thought: Looks like she found a better piece of work than us. It occurred to him that the difference might be in the man, even though this didn't make a lot of sense, because he seemed as hard as the rest of his mother's life, which had never seemed so hard until now that he saw her in command. Looking out at the long stretch of grass outside the window and then the trees in cloudy sunlight, he had to agree with his brother after all, that she'd found a place that she thought she could own. "We never made her happy," he said.

She was sitting on a chair set by the window, looking out, and she didn't even turn her head. John was sitting in another chair right in the middle of the room, staring around. "A person could go crazy here," he said.

At that she turned her face to them, a severe smile on it, and said with her emphatic hands once more, DO NOT.

It had been coming to the woman slowly, now she saw it, that it was not her fault that instead of growing up her boys seemed to grow down. They were made of material tending to weakness instead of strength—it wouldn't hold a shape—and only insofar as the material had come out of her, although she'd never volunteered it, could she take credit or blame for the way they were. She would not even take credit for Doug, though she was going soft about him for a while there, because he was so weak in the face of his brother's good luck in looks that he never even saw that he was the one holding John up.

She had the girl to thank for straightening her out. The girl was wild in her way and she had her contrary times like any creature, but, for all the dumbness and strangeness of her material, she still took a good shape in the woman's hands. The father left her so much alone now that the woman was taking full credit for her these days. The girl took what she was given and did whatever she was shown the way to do, and, when she wasn't given or shown anything, she kept herself busy without feeling the need to do damage except occasionally to her clothes or to herself or some small thing around the house when she tried to give herself a task. What could be weaker than stupid, was how the woman saw it, and stupid was still how she saw the girl because she had to learn everything from the woman, who didn't realize how much the whole civilized world taught a person—but even with such a weakness, the girl managed to grow up.

As the girl was growing up, the woman was thinking that, stupid or not, she would make a good wife, which she had always considered the successful end of womanhood. But now that she was taking credit for the girl, the woman was not so sure. She was so impressed with her own good influence that she began to wonder about any other influences, such as the ones that came to bear on a woman forced to have weak children like her own. She began to wonder if the girl wasn't better off left to her.

She was so impressed with the new power of her influence that, instead of introducing the boys to the notion of the girl, pointing them at trouble by warning them away, she only told them to stay where they were and thought they would, although they never had before; but then again never before had they been able to see how their lives, if nothing else, depended on her. And in her strange new certainty it was true they got a scare.

In the morning, which his brother slept away, Doug was sitting at the window, studying the expanse of land and wondering how it was that in so wide a world he always ended up confined to such small rooms. He was contemplating how it would be to have land like this without hiding, contemplating also how it could be, when he saw the girl. She was walking through the trees, close enough for him to see a pattern on her dress, although not what it was, and the hop her one braid made every time she took a step, barefoot. She looked to be high-school age, maybe half his, though there was something a bit off, he didn't know what, except that the dress and bare feet figured in the feeling. In the shade the girl was a shadow, but when she went through a patch of light her hair and bare arm and blue dress shone for just a second, like a flash. Then she walked on, in the shade again, without once looking at the cabin, as if it were no more than another tree that she was used to passing.

So this was his mother's work that weakened her need of sons. She had a girl to look after. Despite the bright look, it struck him that the girl was sick, or why else would she need a caretaker, but then, because he had been dwelling on the wealth of all the land around, so strange to him, he also thought it just might be that children of the rich sometimes had to be watched like this, unless she was the man's young wife, but that seemed unlikely, too. He couldn't see his mother caretaking a wife, in view of how she took John's part whenever a wife was involved.

Then his brother stirred in bed and a sick feeling came over him. John propped himself up on one elbow and looked across the room at him and, in his way of showing interest only when it was in everybody else's interest that he didn't, as he normally didn't, said, "What are you looking at?"

"Nothing," Doug said and turned back.

"Yeah," his brother said. "A person could go crazy around here."

Doug waited for his mother to come to the cabin. He was afraid of running into the girl. Two days passed before she came back with a new supply of food, when John happened to be out in the woods looking for worms—he had a plan to go fishing, going only on the notion that so big a place as this must have some water on it. Doug could see him through the window, digging in the dirt under the trees where the girl had been, and, keeping watch, he asked his mother, "What about that girl?"

She stamped her foot to make him turn around, and when he did her face was furious. DO NOT, she told him with that flat hand cutting through the air, DO NOT. He went to her and took her hand, which didn't soften in his own.

He said, "I only saw her."

She slapped the flat of her free hand against her chest in a demanding way that was entirely new to him.

"Sick?" he said, and she tipped her head, her hard look still in place, as if she either didn't understand or couldn't fashion a subtle enough answer. "Look," he said, "I couldn't help seeing her, could I? She was right there." He nodded out the window at where John was digging. Following his look, his mother's face went blank, as if what she saw started a thought demanding all of her attention, even the little that looking out required.

Though he watched most mornings after that, the girl didn't appear again, and he kept thinking of his mother's nonanswer when he'd asked her, "Sick?"

John had his hand turned up against the sun, which seemed to angle right at his eyes, when he topped a hill and almost stumbled on the girl. He stopped just short of stepping on her. She was sprawled out on the grass asleep. First he had to comprehend her, girl, and then he had to consider all the angles of the situation with suspicion to match his surprise, because he was so used to the place by now that anything he didn't know about it had to be a trick, so when he got back to her his mind was in the devious mode that suspicion induced.

He had the advantage of being awake, so he didn't have to make any move at all just yet. The women he preferred were of a certain provocative type that at the moment might be apt to make him wary, because it was a woman of this type who'd landed him here in such exile that even a schoolgirl could look good. What he liked in a woman could be seen in suggestive eyes and pouting lips and dresses tight enough to show exactly what was at stake, but he hadn't had any kind of woman for so long that he could see what he liked even in a girl like this. Her sleep and her long brown braid and plain old dress made her look as easy as an idiot, which had its appeal.

Then it occurred to him that this girl must be what his mother was hiding, because she must be hiding something or else she wouldn't be so strange, and the pleasure of finding out a secret added just the edge the easiness needed to provoke him. Already he concluded that the girl, who looked to be sixteen or so, must be the daughter of the man who owned everything around, and that completed the picture.

An opportunity played out in his mind whereby he could get the better of the girl and the man, too. He could knock her up and then he would be roped into a wedding, because what father would want a daughter with a baby and no man around? And what could a man do to the father of his own grandchild? Then a shadow of the man's look came over John for just a second, darkening what hadn't been a plan in the first place, only a notion of doing what he liked with the girl, not that she looked good enough, and even getting money out of it, so now he could see how he would get trapped in it, the girl with the dumb look coming after him whenever she wanted, until he would be all used up. The thought infuriated him and with his boot he knocked one of the girl's bare feet aside.

Her eyes opened, she took a long look at him—and then she made one of the most horrible sounds that he had ever heard from a human, a kind of caw that started deep down in the throat and stopped him where he was, bent over her. As he hovered, she stared at him like an animal, and like an animal she turned her head ever so slightly and watched him from the corner of her eye, as if all her body, sprawled as it had been in sleep, was gathering to spring. He moved, easing his back, and she tensed. That brought on his interest again. It started to seem like a contest. He crouched, a foot between her legs, and reached for the front of her dress.

The sound that came from her then was like the first but worse, a shriek of horror that he could feel at every point where they were touching, and then under his weakened hold the girl seemed to erupt, her body arching like something possessed and lifting him. He fell aside and watched amazed as she scrambled up and ran away, arms thrown back and wild, like someone running from a fire. At the point where the grass met the woods, she suddenly stopped and looked back at him. He was sprawled out as he'd fallen, like a man dropped out of the sky. With all the care he would have shown a crowd, he gathered himself in and sat up as if nothing had ever happened.

Handsome as he was and used to being chased by women, he calculated ways of bringing his charm to bear on the wild girl, but the nature of his customary luck, which required immediate action and then generally turned bad, made him as impatient as he was confident and anyway he could already see the need to hurry past any chance for another scare; so he quickly dismissed all the possibilities that occurred to him, because they all began with looking good and he couldn't figure out how to get the girl to see that when he'd already made her look away. Instead he decided to go right to the part where a girl appreciated a good-looking man coming for her. Then she would see. And maybe this was how to get a girl to keep looking, past the usual turning point.

That night he told his brother. There was a girl out here, he said. That was the big secret.

"Big secret?" his brother wanted to know.

"Yeah, a girl," John said. So wild she had to be kept out here on a game preserve, and that explained a lot. But like all wild things this one wanted to be tamed—more than to be shot, you could be sure of that—and he looked like the one to do it. It was time he did a good deed anyway.

How did he figure? his brother wanted to know then. He was the ugly one—even his name, Doug, had some of ugly in it—which was why he'd grown up to be ambiguous like this, so a person couldn't say whether he wanted to know more about the wildness or the taming or the timing of good deeds.

"How I figure anything," John said, his own name like a pope's or king's, depending, and he tapped his head where the crown would be and figuring happened.

"You talked to her?" Doug said, and John made the face he had for nice points.

"I said she was a wild thing, didn't I?" he said, but he was thinking that Doug didn't seem surprised enough about the girl, as if he was already in on everything.

"You weren't supposed to talk to her," Doug said. "You're supposed to hide."

"Supposed to? Who said?"

"She told us in her way," Doug said. He meant his mother, who he always thought was clear even without speaking, but John could read her many ways. In fact, he had gone through a time of thinking that she didn't speak just so he could learn the world on his own and bring back reports to her and whenever things didn't work out then she could comfort him with no blame to herself. This was the way with mothers if they wanted to keep their children.

"Why do you think she has us here?" he said, and now he saw how the girl was in a way his mother's, too, left alone to learn the world like him.

"Because there's nowhere else to go," Doug said. "And she's our mother."

John saw this nowhere else in quite another way; it meant that a force of fate had brought him to the girl. But because his brother was the one, out of ugliness, always to believe fate put him in the way of things to show him what wasn't allowed, he didn't say another word about his plan, which Doug would make as ugly as he was, which was his way of evening out his chances in such a good-looking world.

After the first fright the girl did not know what to make of the man. She was completely unused to strangers, so his likeness to her father, in that they were both men, struck her deeper than his strangeness, and she didn't know what this meant, whether he was a fake to be fought for trying to take her father's place or just another one of him to be treated the same. Already she was worried that she'd done wrong and her father wouldn't come back again and show her what was right, and if he did come back but didn't show her, she wouldn't know how to find out from him. The man also might have come from her father, from the other place, and it was possible that she would not find out anything from him ever again. This was the hardest thought of all, since the man had reached for her breasts right away, which meant that she might already have earned nothing but punishment, all new rules with the new man, or she might already have frightened his niceness away, because she had acted too fast or slow, and now she wouldn't have anyone, all because she didn't know, and now she still didn't.

That night and the next the man came into her dreams and woke her up. Her sleep didn't know what else to do with him once he'd appeared.

Doug woke to the sound of his brother creeping out of bed. In the wan moonlight, he watched John stealthily dress and then, as he pulled his boots on, slide a look his way, as if even a glance might wake a man, and so he knew his brother's mind, which went the way of trouble naturally but was tending to outright wrong if he considered it worth hiding. When John sneaked out of the room, pretending that he wasn't making the noise a big man like him couldn't help making, Doug got up and watched out the window as his brother headed off, and then he hurried to dress, too. By the time he got outside his brother had disappeared, but, following the way he'd gone, Doug found the main house, silent and dark.

John was already inside, if this was where he'd come, as Doug was just about sure it was, because he'd noticed John sneaking looks ever since he'd encountered the girl, and this must be where she was, his mother, too. By all rights John couldn't have known the layout of the house either, but he had a nose like an animal's for female scent, so when Doug heard a creaking overhead he knew that was where the girl was, with his brother, and he went softly up the stairs.

It was pure dark up there, with no one he could hear or see or smell in the hallway. He felt his way past one silent door and then another, and then he thought he heard something somewhere behind him, so he let himself into the next. His own soundlessness unnerved him as it always did because he couldn't get used to—despite his equal size—being less certainly placed on the earth than John, which was the only explanation he had for the ease with which he went here and there, following his brother's solid noise, as if he needed to be anchored by John's movement, however disreputable.

Now he heard the sound behind him again, so he stood aside and felt more than saw the door opening next to him. There was his brother. He sensed the bulk. Then he heard a stirring and he knew they'd found the girl.

It was as dark here as the hall, so dark he couldn't even tell where there was a shutter or blind or perhaps another whole room between them and the moonlight, but he was sure the girl was getting up. Though he and John were both standing in silence, the girl had clearly awakened and felt them there. Rising, she was whimpering in fear, a weird animal sound like one he'd once heard a deaf woman make when John had started shouting at her because he thought she was mocking his conversation instead of just trying to understand it—and just as had happened then, John froze now; Doug could feel the stiffening two or three feet away as surely as if he had seen it. The girl came through the dark right toward them. The sound she started making as she approached would have been a shriek if it had been any louder. When she'd come halfway, John surprised him by opening the door behind him and backing out.

Doug didn't know whether the girl had seen or heard or felt any or all of this, and when she reached for the door he didn't know if she was pursuing or going for help, so he caught at her, found and clasped her reaching hand to stop her.

The sound she made then gave him the strange feeling of being in his brother's roomy skin, where, however, there was no room for anything unearthly, so to comfort himself as much as the girl he found himself saying softly, clinging to her as she struggled, "It's all right, don't be afraid, nothing bad is going to happen."

Her silence and stillness were sudden and complete. This frightened him almost as much as the other because he had his arms around her and feared that what he felt was tensing, the girl about to burst out in a worse wildness that he wouldn't be able to hold. They stood like that for a few seconds. Cautiously, he touched her hair and then, truly feeling her tense in his arm, patted her head as he used to do with jumpy animals when he was a child, his own touch not much less jumpy. She smelled a little like the outdoors, the smell of earthy grass or leaves. He was suddenly aware of the soft cloth of her nightgown. Wrapped around her middle where he'd caught her, his hand slipped on the curve of her ribs, and now he was aware of her breasts above and her belly below, how close his touch was to everything he thought of when he thought of naked women. He wasn't used to women; first his ugliness discouraged them and then the unpleasantness of his brother's success convinced him of the ugliness of the whole enterprise anyway; so the feel of his hand on the girl's body and the thrill it started disturbed him, since he'd come to protect her only to find himself inside his brother's skin again—that was the greediness he felt for finding the girl's flesh under the cloth that was so thin he thought he could touch her skin right through it. "Don't be afraid," he said again. "It's all right, don't be afraid."

That brought him back to himself. He remembered that he was looking out for the girl, but for John, too, and his mother, whose life they all were, though especially the girl, who was also her livelihood.

"Go back to bed," he said, but the girl didn't move, even when he let his arm fall and she was standing free. He nudged her, but that didn't move her either, and he thought he sensed confusion in her, but he wasn't sure because she was so strange to him, nothing like his brother. Finally he had to circle her waist with his arm in a more fatherly or brotherly way and lead her back to bed.

It took him a second thought to realize that, because he couldn't see and didn't know where he was going, the girl must be helping him. But when they got to the bed she stood next to it, unmoving again. He pushed her, nearly had to shove her, to sit and then lie down, and then he groped for the blankets and covered her.

There was no telling what the girl was thinking, but her quiet way once she was lying down, letting him tuck her in, which seemed like nothing but trust, made him feel even better than himself, a good man. He bent to kiss her good night, not knowing where exactly and finding her soft cheek.

The girl lay awake amazed and trying to recall him.

He was more like an animal than her father. First he had been fierce to test her, when he found her sleeping in his territory, except that it was her territory, too, which he might instead have been trying to claim when he kicked her foot and tried to start to open her dress. She'd frightened him away with her cry but he could see that she wasn't going to attack and so he'd come back to befriend her in the dark, where she couldn't see him making up for the first approach. This was behavior she could understand. It suited her sense of changes that happened when she wasn't watching.

What surprised her was the warmth. She had forgotten it because her father hardly touched her anymore, when he appeared, which wasn't often now either, and so she thought the warmth was just her lonely skin remembering more than she thought she'd forgotten. This was a different one from her father, though, because he made such pleasing sounds as she had never heard, along with the stroking of her hair, which was the touch of happiness, and his face that she recalled and had been seeing in her dreams was also pleasing, like her father's but not like it, too, like the faces she could draw as the old woman did, lines and shapes that were eyes and nose and mouth neatly put together as the old woman's blurry ones weren't and as the girl thought hers weren't either, because they were of the same type, she and the old woman.

When he got back to the cabin John was surprised to find his brother's bed empty, and then he became suspicious. Waiting till I'm gone then sneaking out, was how he saw it, all of a piece with how Doug hadn't been surprised to hear about the girl and how he hadn't wanted him to talk to her, and suddenly it was clear to him that his brother and his mother were up to something, probably working together to deprive him of the girl, which might explain the way she'd leapt away from him, the two of them telling her about the bad turn in his luck. His only people to count on in the world, and they were turning, too.

When he heard the door he lay down with his eyes slitted and watched Doug sneak into the room and crawl into his bed in the silent way he'd been perfecting all these years in hope of just such a chance to steal his brother's luck.

No girl had ever been so soft with him. No girl had ever been with him at all, close enough to be kissed. Doug touched his cheek as if she had kissed him instead of the other way around—and John said she was wild—he had probably scared her, earning an outburst, but that was odd, too, with her so quiet, but then again his brother would say anything about a woman he was contemplating. As soon as he thought of it, this seemed like an important difference between him and his brother, that where he saw a girl, John saw a woman.

Her silence came over him again like a spell, but then her whimpering came back to him, too, and he remembered what he'd wondered, whether she was sick and, if so, how. He wished he could see her—but that broke the spell, her trust, because if he could see her then she could see him and if she could see him then she could see another important difference between him and his brother, one that never worked out in his favor, which was why no girl had ever been so soft with him, or soft at all. No girl could forget his face long enough to let the rest of him approach. He thought this girl was different because she didn't have to see him, but he didn't know how different that was, whether she wouldn't mind or didn't mind so far simply because she hadn't seen him. He was afraid to find out. The trust of her just standing there while he petted her hair had felt too good for him to want to put it to a risky test.

It seemed that in her stillness and her silence the girl might have been listening to another sense, what felt like tension for a moment but was really instinct telling her, conducting it through her skin, that he was there to help her. The trust was something that he'd earned. He considered means of adding to it, nothing he could do for her that might expose his face but maybe something in the world that she might not see but still would let him know that he deserved to be trusted by such a trusting girl. However, going out to do something would mean leaving John unchecked, and now he saw how his brother's bent for trouble served him.

He began to fix the little house, which didn't really need fixing, so he only fixed it up, did some patching and some painting and some hammering together of wobbly furniture, and then, for lack of anything else to do, he went out and fetched water and split wood. John watched as if he were a prisoner plotting a breakout. When he got to the wood, John stood by without raising a hand and after watching a few strokes said, "Only I'm supposed to hide?"

"That what you're doing there?" Doug asked him. "Hiding?"

John said, "I'm sure not bringing down the roof with so much noise."

"How far can it carry?" Doug said. "That girl you saw, the wild one. Does she stay inside?"

"Inside?"

"The house?"

"The house?"

"The other house, the big one, where you know our mother goes."

"Inside?"

"Inside the house," Doug said. "Is that where the girl goes, too?"

"How do I know. Hiding and all, it's hard to say who goes inside."

Doug tried to make light of his interest, hitting wood. "I mean," he said, "Where did you see her?"

"Around," John said. "Lying around. Like a little wild slut." Doug brought the axe down again, making a clean split, and it was true, the sound rang out, maybe loud enough to reach the house but certainly the woods around, where the girl might well be lying. Like a little slut, his brother had said, and did a slut trust anyone, or trust just anyone, Doug didn't know. As far as he knew, sluts only trusted John, but that might be because John was the only one who could get close to them.

It was like a question that he had to ask the girl, the feeling John brought on, talking like that, so Doug lay waiting in bed that night until his brother was asleep, and then he got up silently and after standing for a minute listening for any change in his brother's heavy breathing he headed for the house.

It was a mystery where his mother was, one of these rooms. In the house, with her nearby, and with his feeling for the girl, as if he were here to make certain that she was not a slut, he was sure of the old woman's warmth as he hadn't been for all the days that they'd been here. This was what it felt like to be a mother, was what he thought, with everyone around you sleeping.

In the dark he found the door and hesitated, all at once wondering what he really wanted to find out, because the feel of the girl had just come back to him, the way she held still with his arm around her, a softening in the dark. He wanted to slip in again and have her come up to him at the door and let him ease her over to the bed just like the last time, giving him back the feeling he already had, as if it was his trust now instead of hers.

He went inside. She was awake, he knew it, but she didn't move. "Don't be afraid," he whispered, but then he didn't know if that made her easy or only more afraid, because she was as still and silent as before. What if she wasn't awake, then woke up hearing a man? he thought. "It's only me," he whispered.

Feeling his way, he found the bed. "I don't know your name," he said. She didn't answer. He was sure he felt her lying there, staring up at him, but when, measuring the bed's position with his knee and guessing hers, he tried to sit down next to her, he sat down right against her instead and shifted quickly, even before it occurred to him that she hadn't moved away. This thrilled him. Then he thought: Something's wrong with her.

It was enough to make him stand up again, uncertain, wishing there were just some way to reenact the first scene at the door, though this was impossible with the girl lying down, and, while he worried over whether he should kiss her cheek again and go and leave it till another time when he would know enough to wait longer at the door, the girl reached out and touched his leg. Her touch struck him as one of placement, feeling where he was, but when it found him, her hand lay on his leg like a faith healer's, not moving or holding or pushing him away, just lying there. He didn't know what to do. After a minute of deliberation, he covered it with his. Then he enfolded it and, holding it, lowered himself onto the bed again. He whispered, "Won't you tell me what your name is?"

Even though she was the one lying down and he was in the position of comforting, he felt faintly convalescent, in the grip of her confidence. With his free hand, he tried to find her face. He touched her hair, then traced his fingertips along her temple and her cheek down to her lips and laid them lightly there, saying, "Don't you say anything?" and waiting to see if they moved. It seemed her lack of speech might be the sickness he'd been sure of in one way or another since it had occurred to him. Stroking her hair as he had before, he bent to kiss her cheek, only to feel her hand on his hair doing just as his hand was, in such a tentative way that he had to hold still, as if she were blind, too, learning by touch.

As soon as he stopped moving, so did she. His hand was in her hair, his face was touching hers. He moved and found her mouth and when he kissed her his hand fell onto her shoulder, as if on its own, so the greed it gathered into him to feel the girl against him again, her skin under his hands, surprised him at the same time that it came to him that the girl's mouth wasn't moving under his.

Abruptly he got up, working his hand as if it were asleep, but then he realized he was doing this and let it fall. "I wanted to make sure," he said, and found himself flexing his hand again. "That you're all right."

The words hung in the girl's silence like a lie, although he wasn't sure they were. "I wanted to do something," he said. "I don't know, maybe you know what." Still he got no answer, not a rustle. In the dark he felt himself flushing, going out.

When he crawled back into bed, John's voice came low across the room, "So she is a slut."

For a minute Doug didn't say anything. "The girl?" he said, when he could. "I wouldn't know. And I wouldn't try to find out if I were you or someone might get hurt."

"Little brother, that sounds like a threat."

"It's a possibility," Doug said.

"And to think here I was, pulling for you," John said.

That infuriated Doug more than anything. It made him feel he'd failed and somehow betrayed the girl anyway.

She had done something wrong and he had gone away again with the soft sounds she liked, but now that she had wondered about him twice and each time he had come back she could see him as someone who would return, so she went over the last visit, looking for mistakes and working back and forth around the kiss because she knew that was the thing, because it was where he'd jumped up, but even if that was the problem she didn't know what to do. Back and forth she went, sneaking her hand from her hair down to her shoulder, then tucking her head to lay her open mouth on the back of her hand, like a fish, until she caught the old woman looking at her in a way she had of narrowing her eyes on a thing to make it disappear. The girl had tried the look herself, and so knew that it worked this way.

After that she only practiced the kiss outside. She sucked her hand and left a mark, and she was doing this again, most interested in the bruise, when she looked up and there he was, and so she knew she had it right. She stood waiting and he came right over to her. The sounds he made were higher in the daylight, fierce again, like the first time she'd seen him. She touched his hair and touched his face, just as he had, and then she had her fingers on his mouth, in the way, with hers open to kiss him, but he wanted her to lie down.

She lay down as she did in bed, with her arms at her sides, but the man only stood above looking down, so she reached up and put her hand on his leg, like the last time. He came down like a bear over her, so sudden that she couldn't help starting, but he brought his mouth down on her open one and before she could breath he was working his lips, so she was trying to get air all the time she could have been trying the kiss. His hands were so much faster now, holding her head and then sliding under her waist, pulling her up, that she became confused and suddenly in her confusion she felt his hands undoing her dress.

Before she thought, she made the sound that had scared him once, but he still had his mouth on hers, and his tongue, trying to taste her, so the sound only went into him and his hands only pushed her frantic ones away from trying to cover herself where it hurt, her dress chafing her there ever since her father had shown her that her breasts were bad. Then the man put his mouth on one and sucked her like a cow, and, even as she felt the most amazing thing, as if he were sucking warmth up through her from between her legs, pulling her tight there, like needing air, the sound came out, like none she'd ever heard herself make, and loud.

The man raised his head like an animal harking, and then he looked around. All of a sudden he leapt up, growling, and left her there. She touched her breast, the wet pebble, but the feeling was gone. It had gone with the man.

The girl might be crazy, John was thinking as he walked away, eying the woods: coming on to me like that, then screaming like a wolf as soon as he started what she was asking for, and he didn't even know where Doug was, anywhere around—not that it mattered, not that Doug would do anything but talk about somebody getting hurt, when it could just as well be himself getting hurt as anybody else.

That just the thought of Doug could deter him from what he wanted made him feel deprived of much more than he might have suspected at first. In fact, the more he thought about it, the more he became convinced that the girl's howling was the sound of animal pleasure, and this could be the best thing yet, if his brother didn't ruin it.

The old woman was suspicious of her son, the one whose brain dropped down between his legs when he needed it most. She had seen the girl kissing her own hand, nothing she had learned from the cow or from the dogs or birds, which she sometimes imitated; and this was a good girl, stupid so the woman couldn't blame her and for the first time sided against animal instincts because it didn't seem the girl was bothered by them until the boys arrived. And now it seemed there was another animal order anyway, the two of them surviving fine without the worst urges of motherhood. And after she'd discovered that, here the girl was hiding something from her, which had never happened since their first learning of each other.

So the next time she went to the cabin, the old woman took the gun. She brought a picture of a bear that she had been drawing all day, trying to get it right or at least intelligible. This she pointed out to her sons; then she raised the gun and demonstrated how she'd shot it. Still holding the gun up with one hand, with the heel of the other she rubbed out the picture of the bear.

"Don't point that gun at me," John said to her. "Are you crazy? Because you know you're acting like it. I told you a person could go crazy around here."

Slowly she lowered the gun, leaned it against her, pointing up in the most careless way, which made him disbelieve that she had ever really shot it, and she raised her forefinger, still crooked from fitting to the trigger, as if she could not quite bring herself to point at him. Looking at it out in the air there like a hook, John said, "Didn't we think this was a sweet deal, but you know what's happening here? Women are running wild. And now our mother wants to shoot us, shoot her own bear cubs that she brought into the world. If we have to get shot we could go anywhere and get it and at least we could have some fun first instead of going crazy."

His mother looked over his shoulder at Doug with the trapped expression she wore when she was considering a situation, so he figured he had said exactly the right thing and worried her and she would really rather have them around after all.

Doug said, "She won't shoot us unless she has to."

He couldn't make out his mother's look to a certainty, but he believed it showed that she was as concerned about John making trouble anywhere else as here. He believed it meant: Do I have to shoot him to make him behave?

He couldn't get the girl out of his mind, and now he wondered what she'd told his mother to make her so mad, when he'd only kissed her, even if he'd wanted to do more. The problem as he saw it was that if his hand on the girl's shoulder had told her that much, then his going away should have told her the rest, that his feeling for her was careful and anything she didn't want he didn't want either, at least not enough to force. But it was possible that the girl knew better than he did. It was possible that she knew what he wasn't aware of, or that she'd never even wanted him to kiss her, even though she'd touched his face in what seemed like such a wishful way.

When he went back to her, it was to be sure again. He couldn't see how he could think about her so much without the girl knowing it. She was just in his thoughts too much for him to claim them as only his own.

Now that the old woman knew to be watchful, she was sleeping half-awake; so this time when the door opened downstairs she heard it. Lying in bed, she listened to the footsteps on the stairs, so soft that she wondered for a second if she had been wrong and there was someone else, a stranger here, because she knew John didn't have the wherewithal to be so quiet. He didn't have the shame. She eased out of bed and crept to her door, which was not latched, and when the steps went past she opened it a crack and peered out at the back of the man moving down the hall. It had never occurred to her that the culprit might be Doug and so she was stuck for a minute at the door, considering the fact.

There had been that look between them when John said they could go anywhere else and have some fun before getting shot, which she took to mean fun for nobody else but John, and in the way Doug took her look she could see that he agreed that John had had enough of that sort of fun for any son or brother. How Doug could agree with her on that and still be up to trouble, unless he just felt overlooked, was a difficult question, and by now the door was closed behind him. There was no disruption in there. Now she heard nothing at all. Whether Doug even knew how to make trouble for a woman was another difficult question that she'd thought of more than once before, when she'd considered that John had more than his share of manhood in the animal sense and she'd guessed he'd gotten it from Doug, leaving him weak where women were concerned. Then she gave some more thought to the girl kissing her hand and she shut the door and went back to her bed. Who was she, a mother after all, to say that any girl, even a stupid one, shouldn't have a chance to know what a man was? He was a man, wasn't he?

"It's me," he whispered in the dark, but didn't get an answer. He went right to the bed and stood there for a minute looking down into the dark. "What do you want?" he said. "I got to know. Do you want me to go away?"

She didn't say. He sat down on the bed and waited for the sound of John saying *and I was pulling for you* to go away, all the while aware of the pull of the girl as if just her presence there was begging him to listen to his brother, as if her breathing body was drawing his senses down. "I can go away," he said. She moved. Her hand traveled up his arm and found his face and touched his lips. Then her other hand began to stroke his hair. Gathering up all of his resistance, he pressed her hand against his lips, but then couldn't hold off anymore, and, with her hand stroking his hair, he buried his face in her neck. He kissed the warm skin there, where he could feel her pulse against his lips, he kissed her chin, her cheek, her forehead, anywhere but her mouth, remembering the stillness last time, but then finding her mouth anyway and feeling her kiss him, in such a clumsy way that he was overcome with love.

Her hand in his hair was pressing him, moving his head down, until he felt the fabric of her gown and her other quick fingers there fumbling the cloth out of the way. This was such a revelation that for an instant it was almost like he could see her, so bright that he closed his eyes against her breast, and then the touch of her soft skin sent a shudder through him and everything was darker than before. His hands were frantic on her, trying to get ahold of her all at once and press her against him everywhere, and his mouth was frantic, too, crushed against her breast, breathing her in, clumsy and greedy as a cub feeding for the first time, while his hands scrambled in the cloth, caught trying to clear it away from her skin. Moving blind, nothing but a need, his hands got wound up in the fabric of her gown, the sheets, he didn't know, and he heard the sound in his throat, like something coming from an animal, as he tried to wrestle them free and at the same time keep them on her, clutching.

The sound startled him into stillness. She answered with one of her own, a soft little sob of breath. He felt her chest rising and falling, her quick heartbeat, under his trapped hands. There was her soft body, lying still and open if he wanted to crush her, which was what he'd wanted, he could feel it even now with his senses returning to him, in return for her sweetness, this wild longing to force all of his strength on her as if it had to be got rid and that was the only way, to crush it out.

"Don't be afraid," he murmured to her but his voice wasn't his own. He was ashamed. This was what John did with women, who were sluts, and sluts were not women you loved. What they did was make a man into a murderer like John if he couldn't crush all of his strength out in them. But what he wanted was to do something good. He wanted to take care of the girl, although he couldn't see a way. "Don't be afraid," he said again, himself again if somewhat shaken. "I'll take care of you."

Feeling righteous, he got up and gave her a kiss of restraint and left the room wondering what he could do.

Inside she was screaming now. Sometimes it built up and escaped in a whimper or a sigh that made the old woman look up from whatever she was doing and regard her with a measuring eye that was new, too, along with lessons in cooking food and sewing the tears in her clothes, as if the woman was teaching her to do what she herself did so she could take over or they could do it together, like two of the old woman.

She didn't know if she was doing right or wrong anymore, what she was being shown, because the pleasure and the punishment were so close it was almost impossible to tell which was which, the lessons from the man that felt good when she took them up, but then left her unhappy after trying.

When she saw the man again, inside the scream turned into the sound the cow made when it was in pain. She pressed her hands against her breasts, watching him walk up to her from the little house where she had found him. When he reached her, she lay down, and, standing over her, he made the daylight sounds, high and fierce. She unbuttoned her dress. The sun on her breasts was warm, like the touch of her own hand when she tried to smooth away the feeling the man left there.

He was undoing his pants, showing her what she had never seen of a man—but this she had seen on a dog, the way the sagging flesh between his legs stiffened and stuck out, though what always followed was something that she'd never been able to see in any connection with herself; it was just what dogs did. Now she was confused. She reached to stroke his hair and bring his face down to her breast as he came down over her like before, but this time he only took her breast in his hand and pressed his thumb into the tip, and, when she strained up to get him to suck on it again, he moved his hands to her raised back and turned her over. Then he pushed her dress up on her back and pulled her hips up in the air, making his noises all the time, and knocked her knees apart with his, so even in the warm air it was cold between her legs. This was what the dogs did, one on top of the other, the one above poking the hard part between his legs against the one below, and that one always howled—and now she did, too, and tried to get away, but his fingers dug into her hips and grabbed her back to where he could stick it into her again.

Doug was coming back to the cabin when he spotted the girl standing on the ridge. He watched her hold herself and made a step to go to her, a step into the light, where he remembered, with the sun warm on his face, the way women would look at him whenever he walked up to them only to ask them something, and then he saw John walking toward the girl. She was holding herself for him.

He watched her lie down and undo her dress and caress John's head, drawing it down to her, and it was like being kicked in the stomach to see his brother handle the girl, but worse, a killing feeling, to see how she arched to him. He watched the girl turn over and he watched John spread her legs and the feeling grew so strong that he started to move again, but he could hardly walk, as if the ugliness was a leaden weight pressing against him with every step he tried to take. Then John was on top of her. Doug felt a furious leaping forward in himself, but he couldn't move at all, he was suddenly made of lead, amazed to feel his cock hardening in his pants and his breathing coming heavy while he couldn't help but watch, couldn't take his eyes off of his brother's brutal sex. He heard the howl and thought it was his own as he fell to the ground and clutched the earth sobbing over his sorry manhood. Slut, he started sobbing, slut, slut, slut, and clutched himself between the legs and rocked himself on the hard ground until the fit passed.

John heard the howl and was enraged because he couldn't batter it away, with all his blood rushing to listen and leaving his cock in a state. He tried again, harder this time, but it wasn't fun anymore since he was aware of everything in the world plucking at him, pulling all of his energy away except the rage to have it over with, to have it right, which couldn't be with so many distractions and the girl limp as a rag doll under him. He could hump a rag doll any time.

She was bleeding. He held her cunt closed on his cock to wipe the blood off when he pulled out of her, hard as when he started and no happier, even worse off. Curling up, the girl covered her cunt with her hand and whimpered, a pitiful sight that made him forget his disgust with everything for a minute, long enough to tell her, "Hey," and pat her hip. He moved her hand and licked the blood around her hole, a big enough man to stretch a woman open like this, to the point of bleeding. Under his mouth, she moaned and he felt the stirring again, maybe a chance to finish it, but then she put her hand down in the way and he got up disgusted, thinking, How could anybody shoot a man after that?

He was just buckling his belt as he got to the cabin door, which flew open in his face, and there was Doug, a look like murder on him for the first time in history. John grinned. His brother was a man after all.

Then Doug slammed the door and, before John knew what was happening even enough to stop grinning, his brother grabbed him by the neck and threw him to the floor and leapt on him. "Hey," John called out, "hey!" He was bigger than Doug, so he was twice surprised, so surprised that he was half-beaten before he even thought to hit back. "Hey," he yelled out, more in triumph than in protest, because he could almost take the last good time the girl denied him out of his brother's rage. "I only did what she was asking me to do. Sucking up to me and pushing her tits in my face. Tight little hole on her, too, nice and tight, so tight a good fucking from a man like me'll make it bleed."

He'd been so intent on yelling this into Doug's face that he wasn't even putting any power into his swings, couldn't anyway because the way his brother took it weakened him with a hateful laugh, knowing that however tight the girl might be he hadn't gotten to the point, but at this last Doug crashed a fist into his face and stunned him into real weakness, deep down where he could feel the real rage gathering up around his disbelief.

"That was a virgin," Doug screamed in his face. "That wasn't a slut, a slut, a slut," he hammered John's head on the ground. "You like bleeding?" he screamed. "See how you like it now."

John had the anger to get up now but he didn't have the strength. The fist he finally lifted met only air, and, looking at it hanging there, he fell back with a loose grin on his baffled face.

Doug left his brother bleeding on the floor and stumbled out into the woods to curl up on the wet ground like a wounded animal and sleep.

The girl was late coming to dinner and she looked like death, pale as if she hadn't slept for days. Running through her tiredness was a tight line of intensity. Every time the old woman looked up, she found her staring at her eyes as if she wanted to ask something but didn't know how. And later when the woman, hearing something odd, came up behind her doing dishes, she discovered the girl muttering, making little cooing noises and then every once in a while what sounded like a word, though she couldn't say what until she understood the girl to utter, "Don't be afraid," in an almost regular fashion compared to the other gibberish but with all the edges slurred. She listened and distinctly heard the girl say it again. She must have been practicing. The words disturbed the woman underneath her pride in such an advance for the poor child, which she thought she had to credit to her son. When her feelings about the words turned into too much of a struggle for her, she made a loud noise, slapping her hands on her apron, and the girl went silent. The woman put her rough hand on the girl's shoulder and what the girl did was unusual, tipping her head to rub her cheek against the woman's hand.

The old woman wasn't used to demonstrations of affection. Love was something she did like everything else, because it was what a person had to do, with her husband once, because he'd married her, as a person had to do, too, then with her boys, because she'd borne them and there was nothing else to do for it; so at the girl's caress she stood for a minute rock-still, seeing nothing that she had to do here, and frowning over it. Then the girl turned in to her, holding her sudsy hands out but burying her face in the woman's neck, like a burrowing infant, and the old woman couldn't help wrapping an arm around her. She patted the girl's braided hair and in her awkward arm and stiff old body felt a softening, as if nature was familiar with this situation, too, and was showing her, as always, what she had to do.

The problem of the embrace was so demanding that it exhausted her and, loosening the girl's hold after enough of that, she was barely able to finish the dishes and the evening chores before taking her up to bed like a sick child. Lifting the lamp at the door as she was about to go out of the room, she looked back a last time at the girl's pale face and saw her eyes watching again in that questioning way. The woman carried the lamp back to the table by the bed. After showing the girl that she was going to leave it there and pointing out a pack of matches, with the sign of warning that she added whenever fire was involved, she extinguished the light and in the dark gave the girl's shoulder another comforting pat.

Doug woke all damp and cold, as if from a terrible dream, his mind knotted around a pain that wasn't clear yet. First he remembered the aching. His whole body was sore from sleeping cramped up in the woods, but that wasn't the worst of it, and then he remembered the rest. That's how you took care of her, was what he thought, seeing again and again, as if this were the punishment, John falling upon the girl like an animal. The pain of it wasn't assuaged at all by the aching he had taken out of John. Every time he saw John forcing himself on the girl the picture slipped back to the one where she was lying back and opening her dress to John and laying her hands on his head, just as she had with him, as if to say she was ready to bleed for whatever man came first or fastest, and again he heard his brother say that he was only doing what she asked. He was doing what she wanted, which was why she'd pulled him down.

Doug didn't know what she wanted, that was the problem—how could he interpret a woman when he never had and she wouldn't tell him in a way he understood? But he knew nobody wanted to be hurt. The girl couldn't have known or she wouldn't have wanted anything from John. Doug saw her confused and suffering, opening her arms to John because she didn't know any better, because a man like himself, who wouldn't hurt a woman, had taught her how to trust a man. He'd taught her that she could touch a man and kiss him and he would be nice to her, so the whole nightmare was really his fault, the girl giving herself to John and John taking her.

Doug dragged himself up in the dark and started walking, each step like moving a weight again, because what he was walking toward kept changing right in front of him, pulling him on and then pushing him back, the girl needing him to comfort her and show her that he could take care of her and at the same time waiting to revile him because he hadn't, because he had done just the opposite and brought John down on her, the girl's soft body that he couldn't get out of his mind, even spread open under John, and her disgust, which he deserved because he was supposed to be in love and still he couldn't help thinking like that. It seemed it would be fair if she hurt him in return, but he couldn't bear the thought of her turning him away now that she was so fixed in his mind, and his confusion made him slow as much as it made him keep moving.

He got so mixed up in his mind that he stopped thinking about how confused the girl might be. So when he went into her room and didn't find her in her bed, after making his painfully slow way over there, and in the more ordinary bafflement of the unexpected finally discovered her in the corner when she whimpered, all of his confusion of anticipation seemed to clear away in surprise, and the problem of her distress wholly occupied his mind again. It called his sympathy up, with simple directions.

She must have been hiding and whimpered in spite of herself, because she was silent now. "It's me," he said, because John was the one who hurt her, "don't be afraid." As he had the first time, when John was there, too, he put an arm around her. He could feel her confusion in the way she let him hold her, careful as he was not to be abrupt, but didn't soften to him. Even lightly as his arm was looped around her, he could feel the tension of her standing away from him inside, a waiting.

Ever so carefully, murmuring to soothe her, he gathered her a little closer, stroked her braided hair, with most of the warmth she conjured up in him turning into reassurance, feeling like a certainty instead of a need in his heart and in his hands, especially when she leaned against him and it seemed like something that she had to tell herself to do and he tightened his arms, telling her, too, it was all right.

In the dark, still murmuring to her not to be afraid, he eased her over to the bed, where he sat down and drew her down onto his lap. Again this was something she allowed more than participated in, sitting almost straight as he tried to nestle her in his arms. "Sorry, I'm wet," he said, because he didn't know if this was some of why she was holding off a little from his attempts to comfort her. He stroked her hair and clumsily caressed her back and kissed her cheek in what he thought was an innocent way that she could understand, and she did give a little in his arms, but still he couldn't tell if she was comforted or only giving in. Then she touched his hair and kissed him, too, in her soft awkward way. The touch was even more tentative than it had been at first and it inspired such a warmth in him and such a regret that now she had to be afraid of him when the only comfort that occurred to him, to hold her closer and tighter, would scare her more. "I'm not like him," he whispered. She touched his face again, blind again, as if she didn't quite believe him, and he couldn't blame her, because she couldn't see his face, a face a person always trusted because the ugliness was so clearly a pain to him, too. "Is there a light?" he said, his mouth close to her ear and breathing in what he thought was her resistance, her silence as she dipped her head, the slight movement of her body in his lap stirring the warmth that confirmed her in her fear, just what he was afraid of. "Is there?" he said. "You can see." With his hand he felt around until he found the bedside table. On it he discovered what he was looking for, a lamp. Shifting the girl with him, he moved closer. The matches out of his pocket were damp and only slurred instead of lighting, but when he ran his hand over the table around the lamp he found another pack. For once, the first time ever that he could think of, his ugliness seemed like an asset, just because it wasn't John's, the difference right there for a girl to see, and he was probably her only comparison.

"You can see, I'm not like him," he said, striking the match, and the girl screamed. The match went out falling from his hand as he grabbed the girl's mouth, stopping the horrible sound, and with his other arm wrenched her down from where she'd leapt up off his lap. She was like an animal struggling in his grasp and in his grasp all the warmth that had gone into comforting her turned back on itself, as if he was the one who needed it now, and his body started demanding it of her, his hands hard on her as if trying to force comfort from her. He covered her mouth with his and gulped the sound and breathed the horror of his ugliness. With one hand holding her down, taking up the shudder from her and feeling it travel down his blood and harden him against her, he shoved her gown up on her legs and searched her flesh until he found the spot that John already knew. "It's all the same to you," he said, "it's all the same," fumbling to open his pants, then prodding her with frantic fingers until he found the opening again. Then he heard the girl's pained sound and the fury went out of him.

In his hands she was still, waiting and defenseless if he wanted to hurt her, only making her small cry of protest as if she couldn't help that either. He bent his head onto her trembling chest. "It is the same," he said. "I am like him. Except not even man enough to go through with being rotten." He smoothed the girls' gown down between them and wrapped her in his arms and caressed her as well as he could until the trembling went out of her. He kissed her face and kissed her fingers and under his careful hands he felt her soften up against him, maybe more weary than she was forgiving. In spite of himself, as he held her in that sleepy way, the wish to have her crept through him again but without any force or fury, with such sweetness that for a moment he was sure that he could have her without hurting her; there was a softness in it somehow all the way from here to there. "I will make it right," he told her. "I swear I will."

The old woman had been lying awake, exhausted by a perplexity that she couldn't even quite pinpoint as to its cause but also unable to sleep because of it, when she heard the stealthy steps on the stairs and knew they were her son's, the lighter one's, and her perplexity increased to the point of pain, but now she had a practical problem to attach it to. He had worn the girl out. This was natural and she remembered now how she herself had gone around wan and drained after learning what a man was about, but she herself had been all there, as the girl obviously was not. She was a stupid, the poor thing. It might be that her constitution was weaker when it came to taking men. But it was also natural for Doug to find out about women after all this time and it might be that a weak constitution was the only kind he could find out from. Though she couldn't see him being like his brother, out to do nothing but damage, she considered that he might not know what a weak constitution could take, having seen the way John's women could take anything, and, after all, he seemed to be teaching the poor girl something, those words, although "Don't be afraid" could go both ways. There was a weakness in it, too, paying out the girl with words so he could learn something off her, when anyone could see the girl was easy enough without words. The old woman flushed for the both of them, two foolish children playing at grownup business.

That was when she heard the scream. She rose up in her bed and dropped her feet onto the floor, but already the sound had stopped as suddenly as it had started.

So Doug wasn't playing after all, was what she thought, and there was some satisfaction in knowing that her son, who always seemed too soft for his own good, didn't have to bribe a woman to get what he wanted from her, now that he knew enough to want it, but with the satisfaction there was just as much distaste because he had to find that out from such a simple girl. She sat there considering, remembering how it was and thinking that there must have been some good in it, getting the boys out of it, but the memory of that particular pain brought back the questioning look of the girl's pale face and the brief scream, and the woman got up and stood there in the dark, listening to the silence of creatures everywhere, and then she sat back down.

Finally she lay down again, heart like a fist, mad at everyone for being so susceptible to nature, herself included.

She woke up with a shame at having lain in bed too long. The shame gave way to anger, so she knew she would have to do something, because her anger was a saving instinct.

She heard someone downstairs and hurried to get dressed and down there, happier to be mad at this breaking of the rules than at any nighttime folly, and there was the owner, the girl's father, as if the angry saving instinct had known what it was about before she ever could have.

She started breakfast for him and, wondering half in worry half in spite where her boys were, went up to wake the girl. The man would have to see that his daughter wasn't herself.

The man didn't understand the woman's language, but she could draw him pictures. She drew one of the girl and then she motioned to the man as if to make the picture go away. He didn't understand, but her drawing wasn't very good, so she tried again, pointing him out and then indicating a shorter person by his side, like family, a daughter, as she demonstrated by showing him the skirt on the stick figure she'd made. Becoming more anxious, she took the picture to the door and threw it out, following it with shooing gestures.

Many looks crossed the man's face in short order. He frowned, but then he heard his daughter's step on the stairs and almost laughed—so he must have mistaken her to mean that the girl had gone away. But as soon as he realized that the girl wasn't gone, another interpretation clearly occurred to him, maybe the right one at last, that he should take the girl away, and his face darkened deep enough to frighten the woman into stopping for the moment. She retrieved the drawing, crumpled it, and dropped it into the stove, which didn't seem to lighten his look any. In the face of such disapproval, she finally understood that she was at fault. She understood that she hadn't done what she was there to do.

The man examined his daughter while she ate her breakfast. She did not look healthy, and the shy eagerness—that might have been a kind of fright, he couldn't tell—in the way she met his eyes no matter how slyly he tried to sneak a look and study her unobserved was even more disturbing to him than her pallor. She seemed to want to tell him something, which could be, it occurred to him, exactly what the old woman didn't want when she told him to throw her out.

As soon as she finished her meal, if what she ate could be called that, he stood and motioned her to follow him into the sitting room. There he closed the door behind her and signaled her to sit down, for the sort of interview that he was almost used to now, as a man in command of money, which seemed to seat so many people with questions and answers before him. However, this was the first time he'd felt the need for an explanation from the girl and so the first time that he'd realized the hardship of such a situation, no means of questioning or answering on either side. The girl did not sit down. His irritation flared. Everything seemed to be out of kilter here, all forms of dumbness conspiring to frustrate him.

Timidly, in a more likely fashion that calmed him somewhat, his daughter came over to him and raised herself on her toes to put her arms around him. He hardly kissed her anymore, much as he missed the sweetness of her baby days, the only days of harmlessness; he hardly visited at all and only gave her the most careful embraces when he did, because in spite of her confinement she was more and more a woman every time he saw her, and all the other women in the world, no matter how far off, put her in danger. He held himself still as she hugged him, his love for her something he had to guard from even the girl herself, and then she kissed him. He could not move. Her lips fluttered over his cheek and fixed on his astonished mouth. She pressed her whole body against him with her fingers in his hair, so he felt the horror coming at him from every direction. Like an animal listening, he stiffened, staring ahead, and then the girl fell back a step and, with that shyly eager look he'd seen all morning, started to unbutton her dress.

The crack of his hand sent her stumbling across the room. She fell against the sofa and slumped on the floor there, her eyes feverish in her flushed face, her dress open, exposing her breast. She touched herself there, as if registering the disgust of his gaze. Then, with the slow and anxious movements of a child in baffling disfavor, she scooted herself down onto the floor, face down, and raised her hips in the air, spreading her knees, and painstakingly, as if expecting punishment, inched her skirt up around her waist.

The sight blinded him. He didn't know what he did or what was happening until he saw his daughter picking herself up off the floor on the other side of the room and running from him, fumbling with the doorknob, then falling out as the door gave and running again. I didn't hurt her, he was thinking, at least I didn't hurt her.

Doug saw the man's car parked by the house and he became aware of his heart hammering as if to hurry encouraging blood to his weary limbs and hold him up through what he had to do. It must have been beating already, since he'd made up his mind to lay his case before his mother, but then the fear had been about what he should do and whether he really should do anything, and now it was about whether he could, so it was settled that he should, and everything was suddenly at stake.

He had spent the night in the woods and knew he was a mess, but the damp earth under the trees had given back to him everything that it had taken out of him the day before, and he could move again, sure of himself if nothing else. Seeing the man's car, he felt the old notions of rightness flitting at him, like tiny demons of neatness and cleanliness and polite speech, which once could make a man stutter and hide, coming to annoy him into nervousness, but they were like nothing to the notion he had now and he brushed through them thinking, Let them go back to the town where they came from, riding, no doubt.

In the kitchen his mother tried to waylay him. For once he couldn't understand her, except that she was putting herself in the way, an old woman confused and fearful and angry all at once, as if it had driven her mad to see that she was not to be his mistress anymore, though how she could know that already was a mystery that he laid at the feet of female intuition, which might master him anyway, if it was that far ahead of him. In her fear he saw success. "Where is he?" he said. She moved to plant herself between him and a door, so he knew the man was in there, and easily he moved her out of the way.

The man was standing in the middle of the room, a dark room circled with old furniture as gnarled and stiff-backed as petrified humans. He didn't turn or move at all when Doug closed the door. "Mister—" Doug said. It occurred to him for the first time that he didn't know the man's name either; so it would be that brutish, but he couldn't help it. "Mister," he said, "look at me," though it was easier to speak to the man's back, and this was what he had to do, because the man wouldn't turn. "I love your daughter."

The effect of this was like the silence after an explosion, the two of them standing there still as creatures startled out of all sound or movement. Doug thought the man must hear his heart. He couldn't understand, because it felt more like an end than a start and that wasn't how it was supposed to be. Then the man turned around and his heart stopped. That was all he knew. It stopped and at the same instant the man's fist crashed into his face and sent him flying, his only thought one of amazed relief: Now I won't have to look at him.

"You," the man bellowed. It was like nothing Doug had ever heard and seemed to come out of another world that opened up around him as he fell. A kick landed in his gut and he folded around it, tried to get up on his hands and knees, but the man broke something across his back and he sprawled out again and couldn't lift himself up when the man started to club him, and after a few more blows he didn't even want to.

"She's mine," the man was screaming now with every swing. "You," he screamed, "love her. Love her, you think you know what it's like," and then he began ripping at Doug's clothes.

He knows, Doug thought. What I am. What I want. Like John. He knows. And instinct made him try to crawl, but all his thoughts were giving in before the man's authority.

Then all at once it stopped.

A silence settled on the room as rich in its own rushing blood as the one before. Doug had barely the strength to turn his head and when he did, wrenching his whole battered frame, all he could see was the man's huge face looming over him, tipped up to look, and his bloody fingers like immense claws clutching handfuls of his shirt and pants. As he looked, the fingers opened.

Doug dropped his head. It hurt too much. Through his pulsing body he could feel the man's rising like a quake. Rested, he turned his head again and stared up on the other side. There was his mother standing at the door, holding the gun. "Shoot," he said, but the sound came out estranged, as if he were shushing her.

He raised up as much as he could and like a crab he crawled sideways, under the gun, falling on his belly a few times before he got to the door. Gripping the frame, he tried to pull himself up. His mother didn't move. She didn't seem to see him there, dragging himself past her feet, so solid in the flat black shoes that they were all he saw as he fell down again and as he felt his way out of the house. When the shot sounded behind him he fell once more, his face kissing the shoes as the image fled before him.

The girl was loping through the woods, her side bent around the soreness where her father had kicked her, one hand holding her bruised face. In her confusion, she had run right past the old woman, but somehow the old woman was before her, too, in the form of the small house where she sometimes went and nobody else. The old woman's warmth the night before was all she had to go on, and she could see the cabin as another embrace, not a chance of hurting her, as the woman never had. Her father either, except that once, showing her to keep her breasts away from him or he would hurt her like today, now she thought she knew—they were for the one who sucked on them, but then he hurt her, too, and she didn't know what to do with the other one, who had only appeared last night.

She had a way of being in the world, good as she understood it, but now suddenly the world was full of problems that she couldn't figure out or even hope to get around without getting hurt first. She bent her head to this and she couldn't believe it. Her past of happiness was too much; it showed her the world meant her well, so now maybe it was only holding out more for her to have. If she could only stop making mistakes and taking lessons wrong, she would get to the happiness where the man's touch and mouth on her were leading, just enough to show her how much she was missing by going the wrong way, into pain. But now she was without help. Her father had always been the one to show her, but now he wouldn't show her anything except how wrong she was going.

Ahead she saw the little house. At once rest looked like the best the world offered her, and then she wondered if this was the good after all, and hurting the lesson, showing the way there.

John heard the door and hoped it was his mother, come to see what had happened to him at his brother's hands, such a good boy. He'd gotten up enough to eat some food and fall down on his cot, where he was waiting to be found.

It was the girl. She didn't look so good herself. For once it wasn't anything he'd done. The surprise on her face was a pleasure to him, containing everything he liked as it did, wariness and hurt, wonder and sympathy, so he was not surprised at all when she made her way over to him, measuring each step against one feeling or another, almost as good as a striptease for bringing back his strength, and then she touched her cautious fingertips to his tender face. "Jesus, I can see again," he said, "I'm raised up from the dead, Lord, watch me walk." The girl's fingers tickled his lips. That was the first he knew how bloated they must be. She sat back on her heels beside the cot and studied him. "What happened to you, honey?" he said. "Same truck that run over me? I know what we can do to show him."

All at once he felt like someone in a hospital bed with arms and legs blown off and nobody telling him yet, because she was so serious on the subject of lust, and it began to irritate him. However, he was in no shape to make her pay the right kind of attention.

She got up off her knees and went, limping a little, to the bowl of water that they used for washing. Dropping the towel into it, she carried the bowl over to the cot and sank down on her knees again. With a gingerly touch, she started wiping off his face.

He held his hand up and she washed that, too, the cloth a solid brown already, lighter when she wrung it out but never to be white again. He tried to open his bloody shirt but fumbled with the buttons until the girl's fingers took over the task. Although the blood was from his face, she started to tend to his chest. Why not? he thought and dropped his hand, much more feebly than it felt, onto his belt buckle—but she remembered that all right and paused and the fear in her face brought his cock up as big as it had to be to inspire such a look, so he decided to undo his belt himself, forgetting how feeble he was.

The girl still hesitated, but he could see that she was listening now, her face alert, and then he heard the stumbling steps, too. "Jesus," he said. "All I have to do is get a hard-on to conjure him up."

Doug flung the door open like a cowboy, though John could see at once that it wasn't an effect he was after. "I didn't think you had it in you, little brother," he said, raising his hand to the girl's bruised face, which was fixed on him in such a desperate way that he had to curse Doug's timing again. "But it looks like she gave you a run for your money. Go ahead and give the boy a lesson," he said to the girl, who'd raised herself up a bit between them, as if to protect him, with his brother looking dumbly on, too weak even to be infuriated, from the look of him. John grinned and drew his belt out of the buckle. Doug took a step. "You know what you want, honey," John said, watching his brother's slow advance, then seeing how Doug kept on coming, "Shit, we can share her."

"No," Doug said. He put his hand on the girl's shoulder and she stiffened. "Get out of the way," he said. "Nobody's going to hurt you." A change came over the girl then. With a strange confounded look, she crept to her feet between them, her eyes shifting and wild. Doug took her by the shoulders and moved her aside.

She stood watching in amazement. There were two voices, she knew them now, the high and fierce one from the cot and the soft one that came to her with soft touches. It had all been words to her, but now she heard the difference and she knew what it meant. This was the lesson of the night that her father had hurt her for misunderstanding.

The one had dropped the other off the bed and now the two of them were rolling on the floor, the voices turning over with them for a minute. Then it went on with only grunting. The hurtful man came up on top. She knew what he would do, it had happened to her, and what she wanted was to save the other one for his soft words and touches, so she threw herself on them.

What followed was confusion, and she was only aware of the

one she wanted putting her aside once more, and then they leapt at each other again, both of them lunging like bears and falling from the weight. She moved around them, looking for a way to stop it, but she couldn't find an opening, they were so close, they seemed to be holding each other up.

Doug felt his brother fall away from him. He stared down at him sitting there on the floor. "Look what my brother did to me," John said. Doug turned around to see his mother standing in the door. Come to save me again, he thought. Then she fired the gun.

Weak as he was, he leapt almost out of his skin. He heard John slump before he saw him, looking down amazed at his stomach where it was blown open. "My mother shot me," he said.

Doug could see the girl rushing to him, her hands reaching out, just touching him as the second shot went off and he tottered and fell, too. He couldn't tell where he was hit but he was sure that he was dead because the numbness was complete to the point of pleasure, the girl bending over him, her hands on his numb face. "Don't be afraid," she was saying, "don't be afraid," over and over, until he couldn't hear it anymore.

The old woman watched the girl stroking her son's face and saying the one thing he'd taught her again and again. With the girl's hands, she mourned this one, who was probably better than the others after all but never good enough to know it. The men seemed better off dead to her. It wasn't like something she'd done. It was more like another fact that laid out work before her, the cleaning up of all this blood, the dragging and the dressing and the burying, and then the care of the girl all alone until she had to die herself and had to hope that the poor thing would know enough to bury her, too.

Near November

In the days before electricity spread from the house to the outbuildings, in the days when their father had carried a lantern through the black morning to the barn, she and Rachel had wanted to wear the same dresses and shoes, to share chores, to sleep in one bed, under whose covers of eyelet and thin wool and down secrets could be told and lost. They had watched Jake milk Bessie and Eunice, and later, Bessie and Molly, and last—had he forgotten that his own daughter's name was Elizabeth?—Molly and Lizzie, then had scrambled up into the loft to await a moment of enough daylight and warmth for the leading of the cows from the barn to grass, their job. Alone, Elizabeth had learned later, after seeing the Durnings' machines milking, that keeping two cows for milk and cream and butter was not a farmer's business but her father's idiosyncrasy.

Now the barn was sided with aluminum and, at the touch of a switch by the door, would fill with a cold, white light. These were Rachel's innovations. Aluminum siding was something that Rachel would believe in. She would have faith in rows of shining white houses and would see behind each undivided picture window a family of four whose lives were ordered around meals cooked in a clean electric oven and blessed by the youngest. Elizabeth ran her hand along the wall until her thumb struck the switch. The fluorescent light, as violent as it was, could not quite penetrate the shadows in the corners, in the loft, in the rafters.

Where would the electricity go, now that the barn was to be planked up and the house closed? Would it travel along the wires overhead to other bright spots while the barn, bare to prying fingers, returned to an old darkness of sighs and rustling straw? But, by then, the farm would belong to Durning, whose property bounded these acres on every side; and wouldn't he raze the barn, and the house, and clear a few more squares of land for planting? Aaron and Slow and the other Durnings would work the land as they had for Jake, then, after his death, for Rachel. At night there would be no sound but the chirping of crickets and a sibilant breeze combing wheat. Elizabeth smiled.

At a sigh behind her, she turned. Slow stood in the doorway, his big hands hanging at his sides. "So sad," he said, as if he could see what she remembered. If so, his sympathy told her that he couldn't understand. At the graveside he had touched her elbow and she had shivered. Aaron had stepped away from his wife and sons to tell her how sorry he was. Then he had put a hand on his brother's shoulder. Elizabeth had been irritated by the Durnings' sadness and the pitying glances that the other mourners gave her.

Slow still had the almost offensive beauty he had had as a boy. His hair was lighter now, and there were fine smile lines at the corners of his eyes and lips. In one of her letters, those uncanny imitations of familial affection, Rachel had described him and said, "I think God has compensated for his clumsiness of mind by giving him grace." And Elizabeth had recognized this as Rachel's attempt to sanctify her friendship with Slow. "What do we do now?" he said.

"Come in," Elizabeth said. "We'll have some tea."

"Yes," he said, "good."

When Elizabeth hesitated at the threshold, Slow did not move. He waited proprietarily until she went out; then he turned out the light and closed and bolted the door.

"Good," he had said, just as her father would have answered her suggestion, a hint of benediction in his nod. She imagined that on the seventh day God had said good much the same way Jake said good to a meal or a pipe or a neat repair. Slow had always been her father's follower. He had copied Jake's dress, mimicked his manner and adopted his odd words. He spoke of the wheat's specificity, the weather's signification. Even his name had come indirectly from Jake.

Until their father corrected them, they had called the boy cruel names learned from other children. "I wouldn't say that, and neither will you,"Jake had said. "He's only slow, and there's nothing wrong with slow." Then they had corrected one another until he was called nothing but Slow.

Once he had turned on them; that wasn't his name, he told them. "Slow," they answered, "Jake said."

" We like you, Slow," Rachel said, as if she knew then that the name was not what hurt him. Though he ran away that time, he never bothered about the name again.

With Slow following at a gait no more solemn on his day of mourning than it always was—she could hear him, could almost see him—Elizabeth went into the house that was now hers as it had never been Jake's or Rachel's. As sure as Slow, the chill came after her, through the doorway, down the hall, into the kitchen. Remembered in this cold, bright room with its windows looking out on acres of darkness, her common days at a desk in an office eighteen stories above the traffic of a city suddenly seemed as exotic as she had once imagined they would be. Nothing in the kitchen had been altered. The table sat in the same corner, the old dishtowels hung from pegs over the sink, the cups were stacked in twos on the cupboard shelf that they had always occupied. She was thankful for Slow, whose marks of age assured her that she had been gone years and was not still her old self standing in a cold room fancying most of her life.

"Sit down," he said.

She did not know when she had opened the cupboard, was not sure how long she had been staring at the nestled pairs of cups. Slow reached past her and took down two. Elizabeth sat at the table and watched as he filled the kettle and stretched to set it on the stove. He must have splashed some water on his hand; he lifted it now to run it lightly down the folds of the dishtowel, just as Rachel would have done, as if there were unnecessary violence in any more vigorous action, a wringing or a rubbing. Elizabeth noted the familiarity with which he took from their places spoons and saucers, tea and sugar. Then, as if to hurry today into the past, he took the calendar off its nail and turned the page to November.

She had been mistaken; everything was not as it had been. Rachel had put her hand on every dish, every cloth, every piece of furniture, every surface.

Slow spoke and startled her. "Everything's going to stay," he said.

He was turned away from her, spooning tea into the pot. When he didn't elaborate, she said, "Stay?"

"How it is."

"How do you know?"

"It's what I'm going to do."

He brought the teapot to the table and laid the cozy next to it. When he was standing at the refrigerator, holding a pitcher of cream under his nose, she said, "Slow, your father's buying the place."

"Yes," he said and smiled, indicating that the cream was fresh, "for me." He put the cream and sugar in front of her. "It's our house."

"Our house?"

He busied himself with the strainer. "Rachel's house," he said, low.

After everything, his loyalty had lasted this long, after the blows he had taken because of her, after the hard attention she'd brought to him. But then, hadn't Rachel tended to his cut lip? Kneeling in the straw beside him, hadn't she smoothed back his hair and kissed his forehead again? From the dark loft Elizabeth had seen them, night after night, Rachel sitting or kneeling close to him, whispering, stroking his hair with her careful hand. He would raise his hand and, with the tips of his fingers, touch the spot she had kissed. In the barn, he gave up being like Jake and, as if his daylong effort at emulating the man had robbed him of the strength it took to stand or sit, he lay on the ground and murmured all his worries to Rachel, who comforted him.

Rachel had a romantic notion of mothering. When Jake had announced that their mother had gone away, Rachel, too young to understand what he was saying, cried anyway.

"Where'd she go?" Elizabeth had asked.

"Away" was as specific as Jake would get.

They had grown up enough to see this as a father's way of telling children that their mother had died—and they had, for some time, accepted her as dead—when she decided to visit. Elizabeth felt fooled and foolish and resisted the woman's embraces. But Rachel hung on her mother's neck and begged her, a near-stranger, not to go away again. Elizabeth and Jake looked at each other. They knew that this demonstration, the tears and hugs she was wasting on her daughters, was for him.

The next day she was gone again. "I'm going to tell you what kind of woman your mother is," Jake said. Then he told them and told them that was enough of that subject. Elizabeth knew that Rachel wasn't old enough to understand that "tramp" could mean hobo or whore. She knew what her mother was, but Rachel never learned.

At the bottom of her letter detailing the funeral arrangements for Jake, she had written in her looping hand, "What to do about the things that are Mother's? They were never divorced." Elizabeth knew how deliberately Rachel, imagining that a postscript could confirm a life of faith in love-and-marriage, had added this remark.

Instead of making her sensible, as it should have, Jake's dismissal of their mother had marked the beginning of Rachel's sentimental misconceptions. Her transformation into a sweet, maternal image of herself seemed to have started then, as if her new understanding would not allow the family to go motherless. Jake only helped to make matters worse. Being a man, and so, as Elizabeth saw it, soft to certain attentions, he encouraged Rachel with his appreciative sighs and nods and words of approbation for every effort she made, basket lunches carried to him when he stayed all day on his tractor, a hammock strung one summer between two oaks, radiator-warmed socks waiting at the end of each winter day, stories read to him after dinner while he rested his eyes. He even approved her adoption of Slow—and every other farm hand and neighbor and grievous soul who found her sooner or later. Rachel was grooming herself for the farm, Elizabeth thought, which Jake would, of course, consider good; if there were to be a continuity, it was somehow right that Rachel should have the confidences of every earthbound, ground-turning boy.

Aaron had not been one of them. Slow's brother but, unlike Slow, smart enough to want to get away, he brought Elizabeth those plans that had nothing to do with the land and its life. He had a fine temper and talked, as no one else had been able to, about what concerned her. While they sat at the table with their heads bent together, Rachel moved around the kitchen, stopping now to offer a slice of pie, a cup of coffee, turning, then, to ask in her simple way how the day had gone, whether the new horse she'd seen was his, and was he a good one?

It seemed that one day Aaron was answering Rachel politely, and the next he was inviting her to sit with them. Elizabeth tired of their conversation. His character was so changeable that, apparently unaware of contradiction, he revised the plans she had admired. Within a month's time, she had to admit to herself that there was nothing but talk in the resolve that had drawn her to him. When he began to arrive asking for Rachel, Elizabeth was relieved. She remembered how relieved she had been.

The last time he asked for her sister, Elizabeth suggested that he try the barn. She could only guess that Rachel would be there, ministering to Slow through the medium of the dark. Her touches must not have seemed innocent to Aaron, for it was shortly after he'd looked for Rachel in the barn, and left quickly, that Elizabeth began to hear about her sister and Slow. That Aaron would spread stories about his own brother had only confirmed her doubts about his character. When what must have been his version of the scene got to her, through second parties and third; she was surprised at the embellishments he had put on Rachel's and Slow's simplicity.

Maybe Rachel, not Slow, had needed comforting afterward, though she'd never admitted to being mistreated, never seemed to acknowledge how unfairly misunderstood she'd been, only smiled her placid smile. Though not spoken of openly, the story was somehow known, and known in a way that gave her generous manner an altogether different aspect. Maybe that, as much as Rachel's need for devotion, had held them together and, even now, kept Slow, as helpless as he was, protective of her. Other than fear and weakness, what would make a person stay?

Elizabeth thought it best to humor Slow. If he wanted to believe that the house would be his and would be, even without Rachel in it, the sanctuary it had been, then to undeceive him today would be unnecessary and unkind, another kind of weakness. "Surely you'll change something," she said.

"Why?"

"Everything preserved—won't it make you think of—."

"Yes." His frown was the frown that Jake had always had for foolish remarks and frivolous women. The look, from Jake, had been his way of acknowledging that they both knew better than whatever had been said and would not waste time pursuing the thought further. She was embarrassed at being silenced by Slow without knowing why and without knowing better. He stood abruptly and said, "I have to change my clothes." As though he were just now realizing that his funeral suit was uncomfortable, he curved his shoulders, straining the cloth of the stiff, black jacket. "Excuse me," he said, and walked to the doorway that led to the stairway.

"Slow," Elizabeth said, "where are you going?"

He turned and studied her for a moment, then, carefully articulating each word, said "I'm going to change my clothes." He pointed to himself. "My suit."

She could hear him climbing the wooden stairs, his tread so steady it seemed that time could be counted against each step. He was overhead, then, but she could not tell whose room he was going into, she did not know what he was doing or why he should come to her house to change his clothes. His confusion at the foot of the stairs, his refusal to explain—or even to see that he had any reason to explain—only made her think of Durning, who had said over the sale that it seemed a natural end to what was happening naturally.

Elizabeth closed her eyes and pictured her apartment. The windows would be white from the radiator's heat and the bright streetlights below. The lamp over her desk would be on and her work, the neat folder of tables that she had brought home, the work that, but for the funeral, would have been today's, would be waiting. The bed was made with fresh linens, the kitchen was clean, the refrigerator was full. She imagined that the phone would ring. Her friend would ask how the trip had gone, and she would tell her that everything was in order.

It was cold here, with no steam to obscure the empty night outside the windows, the black acres that stretched flat all the way to the graveyard where Rachel lay next to Jake and unknown others whose trip to the cemetery had been the farthest journey they had ever made from home. There was silence above.

He had squeezed a drop of detergent into each of their teacups. He had filled them with water and left them in the sink to soak. Rachel had considered it impolite to wash dishes while anyone remained at the table. He had said that nothing would be changed.

Elizabeth put the teapot in the sink and climbed the stairs. She had been in Rachel's room earlier, but, despite her determination to do the necessary ordering of her sister's belongings, she had not touched a thing. The narrow bed, made up so tightly that it seemed sealed, the white, ruffled, voile curtains, the wallpaper with its pattern of rosebuds, all oddly pristine in the bedroom of a forty-two-year old woman, made Elizabeth uncomfortable. Now she looked at the framed newspaper wedding picture hanging above Rachel's dresser. She had heard that she resembled her mother, but she recognized the woman's smile as Rachel's. Straightening, she saw that she had left a handprint in a layer of dust on the dresser top. She opened a drawer. Except for one of Rachel's homemade sachets, the drawer was empty. She picked up the sachet. It had almost no scent.

The other drawers were empty. The closet held only a hatbox and, on hangers, two blouses, one with a frayed collar, the other with a hole in its sleeve.

Elizabeth left the room to look for Slow. The door to Jake's room was open and a light was on. The air in the room was musty with a medicinal odor. Slow, still in his suit, was lying face-down on the bed. As the only concession he ever made to his marriage, as far as she knew, Jake had always slept on one side of his double bed; and it was on this side that Slow was lying now, his left hand holding onto the edge of the mattress, the fingertips of his right touching the other pillow. Stopping on the right side of the bed, Elizabeth looked down at Slow's large, thick-knuckled hand. When she raised her head she could see, at the foot of the closet opposite, the embroidered toes of Rachel's slippers, two small sneakers and three pairs of men's rough work shoes, the rubber soles of one pair crusted around with mud as black as the handful of frozen earth her fingers had broken over Rachel's grave. She had emptied her hand and looked up into all those pitying faces. She remembered them now and saw Rachel's smile, fixed and simple and pitying as all the rest.

Wearily, she sat on the edge of the bed. Looking from Slow's turned head to the black window above him, she remembered the cold, and pressed her hands together for warmth.

Ellen Akins is the author of the novels *Home Movie* (Simon & Schuster) and *Little Woman* (HarperCollins). She is winner of the 1989 Whiting Writer's Award and an Ingram Merrill Foundation Award, as well as a grant from the National Endowment for the Arts. She lives in Cornucopia, Wisconsin, where she is the town constable.